GOLDEN HEART PARADE

STORIES
BY

JOSEPH HOLT

sfwp.com

Library of Congress Cataloging-in-Publication Data
Names: Holt, Joseph, 1980- author.
Title: Golden heart parade : stories / by Joseph Holt.
Description: Santa Fe, NM : Santa Fe Writers Project, [2021] | Summary:
   "The misfits and mavericks in this award-winning story collection shuffle their feet to a
   soundtrack of rumble strips and twangy AM radio. Here, the underdog is king and the
   outsiders are storming the gates. A plucky daughter defends her father by swinging a paint can
   like a mace, teenage renegades sow terror on the highway by throwing cups of root beer, and
   an out-of-work lawyer steamrolls his way through a recreational sports league. For these loners
   and screwballs, the path to redemption is often twisted, heartfelt, and humorous. These stories
   will take you from the karaoke bar to the natural foods co-op, from a city-league broomball game to a broken-down camper in the woods. In lush and lucid prose, Holt explores
   emotional landscapes that reflect the vast terrain of America's heartland. Woven throughout
   is a series of flash-fiction parables, which narrate a journey both exotic and existential. So pull
   up a seat among this motley crew of barflies, road workers, and art school dropouts, and you
   might later find yourself retelling their stories as your own"—Provided by publisher.
Identifiers: LCCN 2020053238 (print) | LCCN 2020053239 (ebook) | ISBN
   9781951631079 (trade paperback) | ISBN 9781951631086 (ebook)
Subjects: LCGFT: Short stories.
Classification: LCC PS3608.O49435956 G65 2021 (print) | LCC
   PS3608.O49435956 (ebook) | DDC 813/.6—dc23
LC record available at https://lccn.loc.gov/2020053238
LC ebook record available at https://lccn.loc.gov/2020053239

Published by SFWP
369 Montezuma Ave. #350
Santa Fe, NM 87501
(505) 428-9045
sfwp.com

Find the author at holt.ink

To my parents, John and Janene,
who afforded me the luxury of art

CONTENTS

WORST AT NIGHT

Our auto-rivet man takes a piston through the bones of his hand and they close the plant two hours early. I need money, but I don't argue. The man's in shock and the floor's a mess with blood. While they wait for an ambulance, our swing-shift manager wraps the man's shoulders with a blanket otherwise used for smothering oil fires. The lines are stopped, production halted. No one says a thing about it, we just grab our jackets and go our separate ways into the night.

Driving home I see my daughter, Sandy, smoking on the stoop of the house where she lives with her mother. Sandy is fifteen. I flash my lights and pull up on the grass—our town is rural enough that the streets have no curbs. Sandy pitches the cigarette and folds a stick of gum in her mouth.

"Where's your mother?" I call from the window of my truck.

"How come you're not at work?"

"There was an accident," I say. "A man got hurt."

Sandy balls up the gum wrapper and flings it into the grass. She comes down the lawn and rests her arms on the ledge of my window.

"It's after midnight," I say. "Where's Rebecca?"

"You're off the beaten path. Are you checking up on me? Mom's out who knows where, by the way. It's just me."

Sandy is light-skinned with freckles and knotty hair pulled back into a ponytail. Over her shoulder, a television glows through the house window. It's often this way, I believe. Many nights I notice Rebecca's car gone from the driveway, even after the bars are closed. Still, I can't do much about it. It's a custody thing. I only stopped tonight having seen Sandy outside.

"You wouldn't believe what Melody Markley said to me today. I hate my friends. It doesn't matter, but I can't sleep," she says. "I'll be late for school tomorrow. Mom already wrote me a note. Do you feel like driving around?"

"No," I say. "I'm going home."

"Take me with."

"Not tonight, girl. It's late."

"Come on, no one's missing me." She squeezes my hand on the wheel, then glides through my headlights and climbs into the cab. "Mom won't care," she says. "Trust me, she won't hardly notice."

What Rebecca thinks no longer matters to me. She and I were never married, though for years we carried on through shouting fits and crying jags. We were volatile, and I was worse. I'd been prone to jealousy and destruction, and once nine or ten years ago I'd bottomed out and split for good, it so happened that keeping distance from Rebecca meant keeping distance from Sandy as well.

"Seatbelt," I say. "And we need to talk about your smoking, miss."

It's fifteen minutes to my place, much of it dirt roads. Sandy tells me how Melody Markley is a junior with dyed-orange hair and three ear piercings. The two of them were friends until Melody had taken to calling Sandy *Marathon*. "Because I still wear a sports bra, like that's a crime," Sandy explains. "And then Heather Burke starts up too, so today in the parking lot I tell them to shut up, and Melody goes if I wanna cry about it I can blow my nose on the tissues in my bra, which isn't true."

I'm not sure how to console her, so I tell her what my father and grandfather told me, that you don't let on when you're hurt, that showing weakness or desperation is only blood in the water to sharks.

"Mom would tell me to steal their boyfriends."

"Rebecca's not the best role model," I say.

"Oh, no shit?"

My land is what you might call a hobby farm—eight head of swine and forty acres of alfalfa. It's family land I've sold away parcel by parcel. Willow trees separate me from the neighboring fields, and bedstraw has overtaken my driveway save for two rutted lines from the wheels of my truck. Tonight it's warm and windless, brightened by a full moon.

Inside, I lean over the kitchen sink with a cold meat sandwich. Sandy sprawls on the living room couch, flipping the pages of an outdoors magazine too fast to process them. "I'm not hungry, thank you," she calls to me. She kicks her boots onto the hardwood floor. In time I join her with a stack of mail, and she curls up her feet to allow me a cushion. "You'd think there's a quota in these magazines for grizzly bear articles," she says, lowering the spine. "Anything good, or just sweepstakes and lawyer bills?"

Someone coughs from inside my bedroom.

Sandy drops her magazine.

"Who is that?" she whispers, sliding up the couch. "Who's here?" Her breath is quick and shallow, like she'd been doused with ice water. I raise a finger to my lips to quiet her. My bedroom is dark, and we can't see anything. Then something squeaks—a floorboard or bedspring, or a whimpering animal.

I hustle Sandy into the kitchen and guide her onto a stool. "Sit still," I say. "Breathe, Sandy." Under the sink I find a dust broom and a half-empty paint can, useless weapons. "Hey—" I whisper, snapping my fingers. "Don't move." I go into the utility closet and grab an old metal softball bat.

In my living room I scan the spaces behind the furniture, look for bulges in the dusty curtains. I take a wide berth until I see my mattress and dresser, my nightstand, moonlight on the trees through the window. I reach around the doorframe and click the bedroom light.

On the floor against the far wall is a fat man lying facedown. He is very fat. He wears canvas jeans and a short leather jacket from which his stomach pools out like he'd been poured there. His hands rest at his waist, swollen as mitts. Even his neck is fat, folding over itself as if looped by wires.

"Get up," I say.

"I'm drunk," says the man.

I prod his kidney with the bat. He squirms in the smallest way, as if burrowing into the floor. "Get up and walk out. My daughter's here."

"I'm drunk," he murmurs. "Untie my boots."

The man's hair is long and thin, draped over his face. He's no one I know. I've never seen anyone so fat. "Who are you?"

"Untie my boots."

I nudge him with my foot, trying to turn him over. "Please don't," he says. "I'm lost." The treads of his boots are caked with mud and straw. He's a pathetic man, sorry and helpless, so I lay down the bat, lift one leg at the ankle, and begin with his boots.

"You stepped in shit," I say. The man fidgets and I lose hold of his laces. Swiftly, with the force of an angry mare, he stomps my chest and pitches me backward. My head strikes the wall, and everything flashes white. The man's hands and knees scrabble the floor, and all at once he launches a shoulder at me, but I dodge him, and he folds into the wall with a grunt.

I pounce and punch him in the ribs, but it's like pummeling a sack of flour. He bucks me off, smothers me, pins my face with his forearm. I grapple for the bat, anything, but my hand only sweeps the dusty floor. The man groans and soughs, and his hair brushes my face, and then I hear—I *feel*, like a firecracker—a solid thud, and the man's weight lifts off me.

I prop myself against the wall, blinking everything into focus. Sandy stands over me, dappled with olive paint, the dented can swinging from her fist. Against the other wall is the fat man, his jacket bunched around his shoulders. He lies motionless, having burst the closet doors from their hinges and collapsed them to splinters.

§

Sandy and I drag the man by his wrists into the living room. His stringy hair parts over his face, revealing acne-scarred cheeks and bulbous lips, an eye that's puffy and crooked from where it absorbed the paint can. And though his breath stinks like meat, or cat food, there's no smell of liquor.

"You shouldna got down to his level," Sandy says. "He said what, untie his boots?"

We drop him in the middle of the room. I tell Sandy to untangle an extension cord from a nearby lamp, which I use to hogtie his ankles. "Now go to the kitchen," I say. "Wrap some ice in a towel and bring a few Tylenol."

"He's unconscious. He'll gag on them."

"Are you kidding?" I say. "For me. I'm the one with a headache."

The man, on his back, makes a clicking noise like he's swallowing his tongue. I tug him onto his side, light shimmering at the corners of my eyes. I give it a moment, then I sift through the man's pockets.

All that's in his jeans are two dimes and a book of matches, a soft pack of unfiltered cigarettes, now flattened. In his jacket I find a roll of twenty-dollar bills—taken from the battery compartment of a baton flashlight in my dresser—and a wax envelope of calf-roping medals worth nothing to anyone but me. In an inside breast pocket is the man's wallet.

"Who is he?"

"I'm a little blurry around the eyes," I say, handing the wallet to Sandy. She gives me the towel and I sit back on the couch. At first the ice only worsens my throbbing head, but then it smoothes out, and I dry-swallow the Tylenol.

"Denny Thorpe," she reads. "Not Dennis, Denny. From Arizona. He's fat for being from Arizona. It says he's five-ten, two-fifty. Well …" She studies the man on the floor. "He's bigger now."

"There's Thorpes around this county. Maybe he's got family here."

Sandy pulls a few other slips from his wallet. "Two cards for auto detailers, a credit thing for 'Dodge City Rentals.' I don't know."

"He's a petty thief," I say, "a penny-ante crook." I tell her about the roll of bills and the rodeo medals. "Men like this keep whatever sticks to their fingers. They scavenge for copper wire and abandon cars when they're out of gas. I know his type. Sandy, don't stand so close to him."

"Should I call the cops?"

"And say what? No, you shouldn't even be here. And I don't exactly want to answer their questions. Let me think."

If indeed Denny Thorpe is a vagabond, he entered my house by chance. Or he could be a goon sicced on me by any number of folks I'd wronged when I'd been at my worst about Rebecca and a terror around town. If that's so, I've already—*we've* already—battered him enough to send a message. We won't turn in Denny Thorpe, but neither will we be around when he awakens.

"Sandy, put your boots on. Do you know Helm and Pearl Thorpe? They live six miles that way. Helm used to run cattle, but now he rents out his land for corn."

"I don't know those guys."

"You don't need to," I say. "They keep to themselves." I explain that we'll drag Denny out and load him in the back of my truck, and we'll dump him at the Thorpe farm. He could be their kin or he could be nobody, but we'll dump him there just the same. What happens after that will be no concern of ours.

§

She and I retrieve a snow sled from the tack barn outside. It's past one now, and the moon glints off the ribbing of my grain bins. I look for Denny's car, truck, or motorcycle, but there is none. One hog whines softly from its pen.

Back inside, we roll Denny onto the sled and lead him out the front of the house. As I'm dragging the sled over the steps, the plastic rim buckles and Denny tumbles down, his face grinding to a halt on the concrete path.

Sandy pops in a stick of gum. "Well, what's another scrape?"

My hand sets off a burning sensation along my arm. I raise it to my face only for blood to scatter the air. The sled, when it buckled, had split the flesh across my palm, leaving a deep crimson gash. "Dad, *shit*—" Sandy rushes inside and returns to fold my hand around a kitchen towel. "Just, hold on." She cinches up the towel with electrical tape, which she then slices with a box cutter from her jeans pocket.

"Where'd that come from?"

"This little razor?" She shifts the dull, rusty blade up and down. "Junk drawer. I was just grabbing things when we first heard the guy."

"Get rid of it," I tell her. "Nothing good will come of that."

Below us, Denny Thorpe groans. He turns to his side on the concrete, but he's only semi-conscious, punch-drunk. I club him with my good fist, and he lets out a small puff of air between his greasy lips.

The sled moves easily across the lawn, parting the tall grass. Sandy takes my keys and reverses the truck along the driveway. "You lift his ankles," I say, dropping the tailgate. "I'll get him by the wrists."

"That is not going to work. We might need a skid steer, or a payloader."

Instead, we yank him upright by his collar until his chin slumps against his chest. Next we try standing him up, but his arms are too doughy to get a handle. "I'll find a rope," I say. "We'll have to make some kind of pulley."

"Wait, let's try this." She squats down and hooks her elbow into Denny's armpit. "Little help here," she says. "Other side." Together we hoist him against the light panel, and I plow him with my shoulder onto the tailgate. "Guess what Melody Markley's doing right now. Probably lying in bed sucking her thumb. No joke, she has to wear a retainer. Are those cigarettes?"

I put my hand to my shirt pocket. "They were in his jeans."

"Well, guess what I found in his sock."

She offers out a four-inch piece of bone—animal bone, with intricate carvings and dark polish in the recesses. It shows a wilderness scene of spruce trees, mountains, and deer. It's a folding knife—a straight razor—thick and hefty, longer even than Sandy's palm. She flicks the steel nub at one end and releases the blade.

"We kinda screwed up," she says. "That coulda been trouble."

"I'll say." I fold the knife closed and slide it in my back pocket. And despite everything, I begin to laugh. "And you thought you stood a chance with a box cutter."

§

I'm securing the tailgate when I hear gravel spinning out along the road. A car passes my driveway and continues maybe fifty feet, then stops and weaves backward in reverse. It turns in with its high beams showing. I crouch beside the truck and yell for Sandy to get down in the cab.

The car—a coupe or mid-size—bottoms out on the ruts and loses the driveway, nearly clipping the front end of my truck. The brake lights flare and it comes to a stop, crookedly, on the concrete pad of my barn.

"Who is it?" Denny says, his voice full of phlegm. I lean over the cargo box and thump him on the temple.

The car is Rebecca's—a two-door Cutlass Ciera, dirty gray, the rear fender collapsed. Ten years back I'd smashed that fender with a shovel when I discovered Rebecca in the backseat with another man.

"I'll handle this," I tell Sandy. "You stay here."

"What about the fat guy?"

Denny is knocked out, foam in the corners of his mouth. "All right," I say, "let's be quick."

Rebecca appears to have lain across the front seat. The dashboard lights put off an orange glow, and the radio plays an outlaw tune with fiddles and smoky baritone. I rap the driver-side window. Rebecca rears up and starts talking. "Turn the music down," I shout. I motion for her to roll down the window.

"There you are," she says. "Terry, you dumb son of a bitch. Sandy, *get* in this car. You're in some shit, little lady. Why's your clothes all green, and what the hell are you grinning at? What's with the mitt, Terry, you dumb shit sack? I don't care. *Get* in the car, Sandy. I am *not* happy. I am pissed."

"Good idea to drive, Mom."

I kill the ignition and throw the keys far off into the grass. "You're here at the wrong time, Rebecca. Go inside and lie down."

"Oh, you lie down. I'll tell you what to do for once." She opens the door and teeters onto her feet. "Huh, what's the meaning?"

I glance back at my truck, where the moonlight glimmers off Denny's leather jacket. "Go inside, Rebecca." But she sweeps her hair from her eyes and folds her arms. "I'm doing you a favor," I say. "I'd just as soon you went and smashed your car into a tree."

"*Dad*," Sandy says, taking her by the wrist. "Come on, Mom. You don't understand."

Rebecca gets a look at Denny Thorpe and trills a low whistle. "That man is F-A-T fat. Who is this piece of shit?"

"He's a Thorpe."

"That don't mean nothing to me."

"Dad, we have to go," Sandy says. "Bring her with."

"No."

"Sure, let's have a convention about it."

"All right, make a decision, Rebecca," I say. "Go inside and sleep it off, or get in the truck and let's go. We'll explain on the way."

Sandy slides the bench forward and tests the pedals, and soon our tires are rumbling over the washboard road. Rebecca sits between us, staring back at Denny Thorpe. She says, "How'd you meet this dude?"

"I *met* him because he was lying in wait on my bedroom floor. He's not what I'd call a friend. He's nobody."

"You ought to lock your doors. I'd wager he didn't sneak through no window."

"No, we think he climbed through the vents," Sandy says.

I turn and check on Denny. His head bounds against the ribs of the truck bed, a jug of antifreeze lodged below his stomach. Plumes of dust spread upward in the red glow of our taillights.

Rebecca starts crying. "What is this?" she says. "This is endangerment. How'd we get here? Sandy, you're supposed to have it better than we did. We're supposed to make better lives for our kids." She wipes her nose on her sleeve. "Sandy, you'll be tough if you survive us. I'm so goddamn angry at you, Terry." She punches me in the chest and cups her hands on her cheeks. "And I know I fucked up worse than you. It's Wednesday night or Thursday night and this is what's become of us."

"Actually, I like this."

"Sandy, promise me this won't happen again."

"This exact thing? It will not happen again."

"Jesus, Rebecca, shut up."

"Here, Mom, have a piece of gum."

Up ahead is the shelterbelt of the Thorpe farm. We're cutting a line between overgrown ditches, past rows of soil recently disked. "Listen, here's what we'll do," I say. "Sandy, cut the lights. You coast up their driveway and park near the house. You and me will step out and leave our doors open—no noise. Rebecca, you keep your ass glued to that seat. I'll drop the tailgate, me and Sandy will tug Denny by his ankles, and we'll be gone before he even hits the ground."

"Okay," Sandy says, nodding. "Roger that."

"Well, is it Denny or Roger?"

"Mom, ass glued to your seat. That's all you need to know."

As we're nearing the Thorpe place, the rear window panel slides open. A meaty fist plunges past Rebecca's head, clutches the rear-view mirror, and rips it from the glass.

"Get down," I shout. Rebecca covers herself and ducks into my lap. "Sandy, scoot!" She slides against the door, her knuckles white on the steering wheel.

In the space between us, Denny Thorpe swings the mirror frame like a hammer. I pound at him with my towel-wrapped hand, and then I curl my arm around his and we lock elbows. His shoulder fills the gap of the window panel, leather squeaking on chrome. Rebecca pries away the mirror, but Denny gropes the air and finds Sandy's ponytail, yanks her in short bursts toward the center of the cab. "*Dad!*"

"Keep straight," I yell. "Eyes forward."

"The knife!"

Before I can reach it, Rebecca howls, twists her body, and bites down on Denny's wrist. He staggers back into the truck bed, his ankles still tied with the extension cord. His hair thrashes in the wind, and he holds out his arms like he's riding a wave.

Sandy then stomps the gas and jerks the wheel. Denny rolls backward against the tailgate, which booms with the volume of a 12-gauge. The gate releases, dumping him onto the gravel behind us. Our tail end swings over and pummels the Thorpes' mailbox, which folds beneath us with a thump. But Sandy jogs the wheel and straightens us out, shifts to neutral, and brings us to a stop without revealing our brake lights. "Tough," she says, making a fist in the air.

A dog barks at the Thorpe house. Their windows light up from the inside. "Drive," I say. "Keep the lights off. Get over this hill." Two yellow Labs appear on the lawn, sniffing around until one catches a scent. It barks twice and the dogs trot, nose down, to where Denny Thorpe must have crawled into the ditch. And soon enough, our truck rolls over the hill and out of sight.

"That enormous man clocked me in the ear," Rebecca says. "I can't hear nothing but the sea."

Within minutes we're back on a paved county road. The moon and stars make the sky like a velvet quilt, and our engine is the only sound for miles. Across the cab, Sandy's face appears cast by shadows. "Hey," I say to her. "I want you to forget this happened."

"I won't talk." She snaps her fingers at me. I pull the cigarettes from my shirt pocket and fling them out the window. "Not the cigarettes," she says. "I want the knife."

(DON'T YOU SEE?)

As a child you were told this joke: there was a blind man in a forest, and he got lost. For years afterward it would breach your thoughts at the oddest of moments, a riddle to be teased, a koan to be unraveled. Later you took to the woods yourself. You traveled trails and footpaths, your feet sinking deep into the mulch. Here were limestone cliffs and duckweed bogs, tiny scattered bones. You learned solitude, if not orienteering. Persistence, you believed, would find you home. Then at once your heart seized with the sound of a foreign chirp, your neck scraped a cluster of needles. The sky above was obscured by branches and tendrils, the sun hidden away beneath gray autumnal clouds. Still, there was plenty of light. You looked for signals, though you knew not the birch from the beech, the aspen from the alder. These days you question not the blind man, but the trees themselves.

SING ALONG

Patterson called to ask if I was in the mood for Applebee's, and I said okay. We both drank a couple margaritas. I got mine blended, and they gave me those sharp, icy daggers to the brain. Patterson spilled forward in his barstool and confessed he'd drank a six-pack already. His breath testified to that truth. Then I excused myself to the men's room, and when I returned he was sitting at a hightop table beside two blonde girls much younger than the both of us.

"Our friend's getting married," the girls said. "We drove all the way from Tempe."

"It's so flat up here," they said. "Our friend studies windmills and energy stuff. Apparently you're hogging all the cool breezes."

"What is that, a berry cooler?" one said to me.

Raspberry margarita, I said. I bought her one. Patterson bought the other girl one with salt on the rim of the glass.

"How old are you?" she asked. "No offense, but you seem old for a foofoo drink."

"Just because it's red doesn't make it foofoo."

"He's old enough not to feel insecure about colorful drinks," Patterson chimed in.

We made our introductions. Both these girls were PR majors, which Patterson and I knew nothing about and went silent when it was our turn to talk. "That means pub-lick rih-lay-shuns," one said.

"I figured it stood for Princess Royalty," said Patterson.

"Excuse me," she said, offering her hands palm-side up. "I'd like to return this big platter of corn. This big block of cheese."

"Come on, that was sweet to say." Her friend looked at me. "How about you say something sweet now?"

"You have nice shoulders," I said too loudly. But it was true. They were dark and meaty and sat well beneath the straps of her tank top.

"Well, I like your hands. I like how they're streaked with white paint. For serious. Are you a painter, like an artist?"

"I paint houses."

"You could probably trim your fingernails, though," she said. "Some guitar players keep long fingernails."

"I cut my fingernails with a buck knife," I said, and felt odd.

Patterson circled his finger for another round. I switched to beer. The ten o'clock news came on the TVs. The girl next to me took out her phone and tapped on the screen.

"Here's what I found. There's karaoke at a place called Jim's—*just* Jim's. Like, is that a bar or some guy's basement?"

"We like karaoke," her friend explained.

"Me and Crumbee are going to Jim's! We were actually going there, weren't we?" Patterson's foot slid off his stool and his elbows thumped the table, sloshing all our drinks.

"I thought you said your name was Kevin."

"Kevin Crumbee," I said. I felt dumb explaining this.

"We like to party," Patterson said convincingly. "Crumbee'll drive."

We finished our drinks and paid the tabs, and then we were outside and I was moving all the newspapers and paint supplies and hamburger wrappers into the hatch of my Camry.

Patterson said from the backseat, "Buckle up, ladies. This chariot goes zero to fifty in just under two minutes."

"It used to have a nylon parachute for decelerating," I said, "but the jet boosters burned holes through it." The girl in shotgun was applying lipstick in the vanity mirror. "That's a nice shade," I told her. "What's it called?"

"We don't have humidity like this in Tempe," she said.

Jim's was actually the scummiest bar in town. I'd sworn it off years ago. Unplanned things happened there. It was in the building that used to be First Rate Pawn & Thrift. Certain walls were still hung with beige pegboard. For a long time, even after it had become Jim's, a bad check I'd tried posting was taped behind the cash register, meant to shame me.

The girls chose a round table up by the karaoke stage. Les Warren was being the emcee. He was a big man with a nice voice. Since it was early and no one had yet signed up, he was handling a Skynyrd song.

"This is what you call a bar here?" said the girl with the shoulders. "Where are we supposed to dance?"

"No shortage of pool tables or dart boards," said her friend.

Patterson left a pitcher of beer on our table. He went and joined Les Warren.

"I know where this is going," I told the girls. "Back to the basics of love." They were paging through the songbook and didn't hear me. On stage, Patterson sang Waylon's part of "Luckenbach, Texas," and Les took Willie Nelson's. The song doesn't require much range, and they did it justice. The dozen or so people clapped for them.

"What're you gonna sing?" asked the girl with the shoulders.

"Probably nothing," I said. "I like listening."

"He used to sing," said Patterson, who'd returned to our table. "Crumbee's got some pipes. He had all the solos in high school choir."

"Back in the Dark Ages," I said. "When our PA system was a paper megaphone."

"We were in a band," Patterson claimed. It seemed to impress the girls. "We were called the Slims, because we wore slim ties. You know that guy from U2, Bono—" he said, pronouncing it wrong. "He was our first drummer. We gave him the boot because we knew we were better than him."

"I thought they were from Ireland."

"He came here for his summers."

The girl with shoulders turned her attention to me. "Why'd you quit singing?"

"I didn't quit," I said. "It's just something I don't do anymore."

"And the difference is what?"

A guy we know called Skunk kneeled down by our table. "What're you purty girls doing with these scuzzbags?" Skunk's black hair had gone fully white at the temples before we'd even hit our twenties. "What d'you scuzzbags plan on doing to these purty girls?"

"Go away, Leslie," said Patterson. "We're having a time here without you. Go sing a song about how you got fired from the wastewater plant for living in the supply closet one month."

"Wife tossed me out," Skunk explained. "Parents wouldn't have me. I didn't know it would last a month."

"His hair … they should call him Skunk," whispered one of the girls, and it made me feel happy.

I said, "You didn't tell me, what are you gonna sing?"

"Pop, pop, pop—pop music." She handed a few song slips to Les Warren.

I bought the next pitcher. The girls went up and made a duet of a Whitney Houston song. It was fine. They were enjoying themselves. They got an admiring round of applause from all the men at Jim's.

When they sat back at the table, they downed their beers. "Whew," one said. "The first time's always sorta scary. Like, what if I'm rusty?"

"To courage." Patterson held up his glass to cheers. "Even better, let's do some shots!"

"Even worse," the girls said. "We're in the mood for foofoo."

The bartender was an old girlfriend of mine named Greta Fettig.

We'd dated briefly in high school. I had once felt her stomach on the knoll by the soccer fields, though I doubt she remembered. Greta said to the girls, "You want what, Sunshine Slammers?" She went to her Bartender's Bible.

The girls came back with tall hurricane glasses filled with pink and orange. Greta had put curly straws and little umbrellas in them. "Get this," one girl said. "They don't have kiwi slices, so she asked if we wanted olives. Like, those two things are way different!"

"We have a girlfriend who tried out for that karaoke TV show," the one girl said to me. "She sang 'Jump' by Van Halen while bouncing on a pogo stick. That was her deal."

"I remember," I said. "She was wearing a tube top. Her breast was exposed."

"That's right. She's the VP-Character Values of our sorority. Her name's Patricia."

"Pogo Patty," I said. "I remember."

"Yeah, she can go up the stairs, but she can't go down them."

Across the table, Patterson and the other girl were talking over the music. He was making her smile. She leaned in and said something in his ear. Then she handed him the umbrella from her drink, of which he used the toothpick end to scrape a brownish peanut skin from between his teeth.

"What's your deal?" asked the one girl.

"Oh," I said. "Sorry, I'm just quiet."

"No, what's your *thing*? Like, what are you into?"

"Gosh," I said. "I don't know."

"My thing is, I think we should collect all those grocery carts people abandon at the side of the road. They're everywhere. It's so ugly. Maybe I was thinking to start a charity in Maricopa County." Her face had a look of genuine tragedy. "We could have teams return them to the stores, or if they're too banged up we'll melt them down into new carts."

"Or, to go one step further," I said, "you could volunteer at a homeless shelter."

"Are we not talking about the same thing?"

Patterson took the stage and sang "Amarillo by Morning." We clapped. Les Warren called the girls back up, and they sang Alanis Morissette's angry song. Greta Fettig was the "Coal Miner's Daughter." The disbarred lawyer Randy Baker did a song by Run-DMC.

At Jim's you can buy a single cigarette for fifty cents. The girls went out back and shared one.

"That blonde is into me," Patterson said. "I can't let myself get too drunk."

"Rewind four hours," I said.

"Rewind twenty years," he said.

"Or switch to water."

"It'll take a lot of water, at this point of my life."

The girls returned. One said, "Are you constantly amazed that your sky has stars? Not in Tempe, no sir."

"You have limitless eyes," Patterson crooned at her. "I could stare into you all night." But the girls had switched seats, and he was talking to the wrong one.

"Stare into me?" she said. "That's not my deal!"

Another pitcher of beer had found our table. The lights around the bar dimmed. Some toughs in leather jackets sauntered around the pool tables. The songs being sung now were slow, languid ballads, and they had trouble competing with the chatter.

"We need some energy," I said to the group. "Sing us a pop song. Pick one everybody knows."

I was handed the song binder. The other girl leaned over the table with me. "Is your friend safe?" she whispered.

"Patterson? You can trust him."

"No, like, will he make it home safely?"

"Oh," I said. "Usually, yes."

"Because me and Amanda might leave. Are there cabs in this town?"

"That's okay," I said. "I'll drive."

"Me and Amanda were talking, and we don't want you to know which hotel we're staying at. Our boyfriends would flip out just knowing we'd come here with you in the first place."

"Right," I said, nodding. "Wait, I thought you were Amanda."

"I am!" She smiled with her ultra-white teeth. "We're both Amandas! It gets confusing at the sorority, so she's Amanda Two and I'm Amanda Three. Amandas One, Four and Five didn't come to the wedding. And if you think that's bad, you should meet the Britneys!"

The songbook was open to a page marked NEW CHART TOPPERS. We both scanned the titles, but neither of us seemed much interested anymore.

"That girl behind the bar, she's watching you. She might like you, I think."

"Her name's Greta. I owe her money," I explained. "The bar, the building, all over town I owe money."

"Still. You should go talk to her," Amanda said. "She has a nice tooth."

§

Soon the girls left. To where, I didn't know. "What happened?" I said.

"Stuck up. Snobs. Hoity toits." Patterson thumbed his nose. "Freeloaders too."

"None of that's true," I said.

"Their loss. I had a thing for the blonde one."

Skunk knocked his hip into the back of my chair. A wave of beer spilled from his mug onto the thigh of my canvas pants.

"Where'd your purty-looking chicks go? You show 'em your wieners and scare 'em off?"

"Yeah," I said. "We scared them with our wieners."

"You shown 'em your wieners and they run off laughing."

"That's how it happened," I said. "That's what I'm telling you. It was our wieners that did it."

Skunk honked out some laughter. Patterson raised his head from the table. "Some purty-looking chicks get frightened by giant wieners, Leslie. Ain't you don't got no understandin' a that?"

"I'm just having fun, guys." Skunk pulled out a chair and sat. He squinted into the karaoke songbook. "What're you singing, Crumbee? How 'bout this one?"

"Sure thing," I said. "Anything from the Disney page, really."

My type of song, if I was to sing, would be early-to-mid-career Rod Stewart. I've thought about this. Granted, when I'm alone in my apartment listening to LPs, I never play Rod Stewart. His songs do nothing for me. They're bland and undistinguished—which, when it comes to performing, I actually see as a virtue. The songs require no personality, so I could efface myself at the microphone. Yet they're popular enough that people know all the words, so they could sing along from their seats and make it their own.

"Let's sing a song together," Skunk said. "You can pick."

"No, ask Patterson. He might do it." Patterson, though, had closed his eyes and was supporting his chin in the palm of his hand.

"Thing is …" Skunk leaned in and whispered. "I love singing in my truck, er whatever. But I get scared in fronta all these people." He fluttered his eyelashes in a demure sort of way.

"That's tough," I told him. "But I'm not singing."

"Come on," he said. "It'll be fun."

"Ask Greaser Jerry. He's your best friend. Or Donna High Heels sitting lonely at the bar. Behind us, you can ask Randy Baker, or Jason Jundt, or Porkchop, Young Buddy, Danny the Mechanic, or Danny the Hockey Coach. Everyone here in the bar," I said, "everyone here wants to sing, but they're all scared. No one's here to listen, because it all sounds like garbage. Ask anyone to sing with you, Skunk, and they'll say yes. Ask anyone."

"I just ast you and you said no."

My feet were propped up on the chair across from me. Greaser Jerry strutted over from the pool tables, yanked out the chair, and dumped down in it backward.

"Hey Crumbay," he said to me. "Them blondies musta figured out you and Pattuhson is a couple zeroes, hey?"

"I was resting my feet there, Jerry."

"I seen you sitting here with 'em the last hour. Me alone, I'da been dogging 'em both in that time. Heh heh!"

"You show some respect," Patterson commanded, back to life. "Those girls had kind souls." His head drifted back into his hands. "And smokin' tits."

"You think you's something special," Jerry said to me and Patterson. "I ain't seen the both a you for months, maybe years. Then you come in showing off them strange babes. Gets me wondering, these zeroes think they better than us?"

I flipped my hand to show Greaser Jerry he was insignificant. He sneered at me filthily and got up for the pool tables. "You still owe me thirty bucks," he said. Skunk stood to leave with him. "Think about it," he said. "You and me doin' a song together."

But I didn't want to sing. It was simple as that. I didn't want people's eyes on me. Back in my twenties, I spent eighteen months in the state prison. I had broken into places and taken what wasn't mine. I was using substances. Everyone knew about it. Before that I'd been outgoing and visible, and others, in a way, gravitated toward me. But then it was like I'd had this fall from grace. To most people, it came to define me. Afterward, I wanted to be done with things that made me noticeable.

Patterson shivered, put his hand to his mouth, and stood. "I will now go retch."

I went to the bar. "Grody Greta," I said. "How long's it been?"

"Crummy Crumbee. Not long enough. Thought maybe you'd cut town, crippled yourself in an accident, or else just curled up and died."

"So you been thinking about me, you're saying."

"Occasionally," she said, "against my wishes, I'm reminded of you." Greta reached below the bar, rattling glasses and cocktail mixers. She pulled up a spiral-bound notebook, its cover green and worn. On it was written KICKED OUT PEOPLE. "Here's the young Crumbee."

She showed a picture of me from roughly fifteen years ago. My face had been trimmed out of a group photo, and I was smiling to the camera. That hair! Those jawbones! My skin fit my face so accurately. There was a man who could hold the attention of a pretty blonde from Tempe.

"Dreamboat," I said, though below the photo was written *deadbeat*.

"Just wait." Greta turned over pages for Greaser Jerry, Porkchop, and others. She stopped at a more recent photo, taken after my prison days, during a bad streak I'd now passed through. I looked repulsive, I'll admit. I was alone on a bench in the act of shouting, and the photo had me looking terrifically constipated. "Who gave you that black eye?" Greta asked. "Me. You were climbing over the bar suckling the fountain taps."

She flipped ahead. There was Patterson, crouched over the pavement in an alleyway. He seemed scared. The camera flash had him looking like a rabies-bitten racoon. "That black eye," Greta told me. "That's from when he bum-rushed me in your defense. Lowlifes."

"All these wonderful memories," I said. "How about for good time's sake, you give me a drink at the old price?" I was hoping to charm her, because by now all I had was coins.

Greta put the notebook away. "How much you got?" I spilled my pocket onto the bar. She sorted the coins with an index finger, then slid them away and dunked them in her tip jar. "You get water now," she said, scooping ice into a tall glass. "Who were your friends?"

"Young'uns in town for a wedding," I said. "They weren't tough enough for this place. Had to run off."

"Can't blame them." She passed me the water. "Who would choose this?"

We looked around the room. Near the pool tables, Greaser Jerry was standing with his arms thrust out, separating two toughs cursing at one another. By the exit, Jerry the Hockey Coach was ramming his fist against a potato chip machine. One guy lit up a cigarette at his table, and Greta went and smashed it out and poured his drink in his lap. Beside me at the bar, Donna High Heels either growled invitingly or belched.

From the stage, Les Warren said, "Bringing us home—last song of the night. Welcome back the Awesome Amandas." Les was looking down at his monitor, queuing up the track. "Let's hear some clapping for our blonde bombshells."

"They ain't here," shouted Jason Jundt, but no one ever listened to Jason Jundt.

Les started the instrumental track. The song was "We Are the World," by Michael Jackson and Stevie Wonder and everyone else. It was probably older than the Amandas. I recall a time back when Jim's was First Rate Pawn & Thrift, when I'd sold all my cassette tapes for pennies on the dollar, that maxi-single included.

"Awesome Amandas," Les said, holding up the song slip.

People looked around, but the girls were long gone.

And who should stumble up onto the stage then but Skunk. He pumped his fist in the air. "I love this song," he yelled into the squealing microphone. "I like singing," he added. "And Various Artists is mah favorite band!" What got into him, I don't know. But he laid in with the first verse—his timing way off, his timbre all over the board, his expression plain spastic.

Patterson came out from the bathroom and recoiled. It was like Skunk's voice contained actual shrapnel. Patterson looked as if he might be sick again. He swallowed his gum and leaped up to the stage.

I didn't know if he would strangle Skunk with the microphone cord or smash apart Les Warren's sound system. But what he did was, he took the open mic and joined in.

Patterson failed to improve on Skunk's noise. He wailed out, unevenly, like a mangy dog in heat. And what was I to do? I didn't even think about it. I just went for the stage, and I sang. We sang.

"We are the world," Patterson yelled. "I'm Hall, you're Oates. He's the Pointer Sisters."

Greaser Jerry howled in approval. He threw his pool cue on the table and stood next to me. His voice was an annoying sound.

One by one came the rest of Jim's, until the entire place—the barstools, the dart boards, the video lottery machines—was vacant. We crammed up there. Everyone. Looking down from the stage, you could imagine tumbleweed bounding merrily through the empty bar. Chairs were knocked askew, drinks left half-finished. We on stage formed a choir of malcontents and undesirables. What we were doing hardly qualified as singing—caterwauling, maybe. There were moans, groans, and grunts. The most tone-deaf read the words off the monitor, and the most intoxicated hummed.

The front door swung open, and the two Amandas stared in at us. Their faces went white with revulsion. "Blondie, you came back!" Patterson said. Amanda with the shoulders gave a shrug to her friend. Together they weaved through the tables and chairs and climbed up on stage.

"We went to another bar," they said. "We like dancing, too." They squeezed in beside us at the microphones. "We heard you before we opened the door. We thought animals were being tortured."

Our group swayed in unison. Beside me, Patterson went for the kiss with one of the Amandas, and she steered him away with a hand to his chest. He was singing the whole time. The other Amanda let me put my arm around her. I was satisfied with that. And I really let loose. I belted. I roared.

"This song's for you," Patterson called to the empty room. "And you, and you, and you."

The music trailed off.

I looked over to Les Warren. I waved for his attention. "Again," I shouted. It was urgent to me. "We're getting better. Again!"

BARKLEY THE ICE KING

1

He was lucky that when he lost his job there were such great sports on television. For a week or two, maybe longer, he sat idly on his sofa wearing sweatpants and ragged t-shirts, cooking pizzas in the oven and drinking diet soda.

Before that, Barkley was a lawyer—a legal advisor for an electronics retailer called BuyAll. He proofread fine print and signed off with a rubber stamp, and in return he got a corner office and an executive's salary. It was a cushy job, zero oversight. But then things changed. The *Star Tribune* ran an exposé on BuyAll alleging all manner of corruption: deceptive filings, creative accounting, executive privilege. *The Wall Street Journal* picked up the story, then *PBS NewsHour*. Barkley took emails and his phone rang incessantly, yet what dirt he knew wouldn't have filled an index card.

Given time, he recognized his own role in BuyAll's malfeasance: he was an empty suit, a name on the payroll suggesting compliance. He thought about quitting but feared looking guilty. His shiftiness alone was arousing suspicion. Afternoons he hid out in a supply closet, punching the bathroom towels or curled in panic on the floor. When the CFO appeared in his office with a nondisclosure agreement and a hefty severance, Barkley accidentally stabbed himself in the arm with a pen, he was so eager to sign. He cleared his desk then and there, a security guard looming over his shoulder.

Now he was considering a new line of work, though he had nothing in mind. One afternoon in his condo, he created his own personal letterhead: FRANK BARKLEY in large, sharp letters. Yet when a 500-count box of stationery arrived in the mail a few days later, he admired it only briefly, stowed it in his desk, and retreated to the kitchen with a newspaper, bypassing the jobs section in favor of sports.

Not since he was a boy collecting cards had Barkley followed sports. For all he knew, Pete Rose was still in good standing and Quebec still had a hockey team. Once he'd gone to college and then law school, got married, passed the bar exam on his fourth attempt, paid down his debt, got divorced, then focused on his career to distract from his personal life, sports had come to seem trivial and unimportant. They were low culture, a pacifier for the masses. But now he'd changed his mind again. Sports were cool. He liked sports. This was the new Frank Barkley, a sports fan.

Freddi called in January to ask if he was free Monday nights. "Monday nights are broomball," she said. "I started a team. You're on the roster." Freddi was an executive assistant from BuyAll who'd also lost her job. She said broomball was like hockey, and Barkley responded she was in luck, because he'd been third line on his high school's JV hockey team. "Oh, super," Freddi said. "I guess that makes you our ringer?"

In broomball, he learned on the internet, you use a bright orange ball the size of a grapefruit, and you wear grippy boots with rubberized soles. The sticks resemble brooms in that they're topped with flat, rubber-molded blades. Games are played in public rinks and city parks, outdoors no matter the temperature. Don't bother looking for broomball on television, the website said—it is a graceless activity for beardos and beer-bellies. It was listed behind only kickball as the second-most pathetic game played by grown-ups.

Freddi's team was called the Icekateers. It included Bogey the BuyAll mailroom worker, Suz the accountant, tax advisors Michelle and Erica Lynn, the sales assistant Darryl Drummond, and a hanger-on named T-Storm who'd either worked for BuyAll or dated someone who had. None of them had played before—broomball, hockey, or maybe any organized sports.

"You stand there," Barkley instructed them at the rink before the first game. "Michelle, go to the red line. You and me can be wingers. Drummond, bend your knees."

"The ice is slippery," said Darryl Drummond.

"No shit. Bogey, are you eating popcorn right now? Tie your goddamn boots."

Erica Lynn took possession on the face-off, but she slipped and fell. An opponent recovered and tried to pass, but he fell. The ball rolled to Freddi, who fell. The only goal came in the second half, when Bogey deflected a loose ball into the Icekateers' own net. "Yes," shouted one of their opponents. "*Goooooal!*" Barkley tried shoulder-checking the man, but he tangled his feet around his own stick and fell.

Later that week, he told his therapist about the game. He described *crashing* the lines, *smashing* the crease, *pounding* the zone. "Frank, listen to your speech," said his therapist. "Your language is brash and violent." But she was ten years younger and from Guatemala, so Barkley dismissed her as ignorant of winter sports. He said broomball to most people was strictly recreational, which is why he would be king of the rink.

"Broomball is not a serious game, Frank. You just said, 'strictly recreational.'"

"Right, for *them*," he said. "For me, it's war."

"That attitude is incorrect," said his therapist. "But it is good to have a hobby." New-age piano music played from a small purple stereo. "Life is more fulfilling when you are passionate about your hobbies. I for one like gardening, and drinking tea."

"I'm gonna stomp rotten ass all over those shithole rinks," Barkley said. "And drinking tea, by the way, doesn't count as a hobby."

His therapist made a note on her canary legal pad. "You are especially confrontational today, Frank."

At the next game, Michelle and Erica Lynn arrived with a set of hand-me-down hockey sweaters, red like hothouse tomatoes, with the words REGAL BUTTE SCHOOL across the chests in iron-on letters. The fabric was pilled and smelled of mothballs, but at least now the Icekateers looked like a team. T-Storm, who was emerging as the team goon, peeled his sweater down to GAL BUTT SC OOL. The letters on Barkley's had been removed already to read GAL UT E.

And Barkley did excel, though not dominate. He tried harder than everyone else, sprawling on his knees and stomach, disrupting passes and unsettling shots. He was a nuisance, an annoyance. He created loose balls that created scrums that created pile-ups. Once, after tripping an opponent near the boards, he was told, "Watch where you're going, douche."

"Blow yourself," Barkley said. "This isn't figure skating."

"It's not the Stanley Cup either."

"If it was, I'd win."

"What?" said the man. "Look at the scoreboard."

"There is no scoreboard, you dumb dick." Barkley made for the ball, but not before hip-checking the man once more into the boards.

And then, in the third game, he scored. He was kneeling with the ball just outside the left circle, when he pump-faked a pass, dribbled across his body, and smacked a wild slapshot. He'd seen a similar move online, in a Canadian broomball montage. In that video, the man's shot had soared over the defense into the top corner of the net. Yet Barkley's swing merely grazed the ball, which spun like a toy top curving in toward the goal. This misdirection sent the goalie scrambling, and she collided into the post and fell. The ball rolled into the net, weakly.

Their opponents responded with two quick, fluky goals. The first came after the face-off while Suz, the Icekateers' goalie, was adjusting the straps on her helmet. For the second, Bogey again deflected the ball into the Icekateers' own net. Barkley hustled to make up the difference.

He scored again, this time by muscling in a rebound from outside the crease. In response, their opponents scored another quick three goals. Game over.

§

Of course, he was often whistled for misconduct. By the fifth game, he'd spent well over an hour in the penalty box. He would spear opponents, trip them, facewash them, one time he even yanked a man's sweater over her his head and tried kneeing him in the stomach, but fell.

He did feel remorse. After each game, he logged his penalties on his personal stationery, an exercise assigned by his therapist. She called it his tantrum diary. And it wasn't just broomball—the diary also told how he'd bullied a salesclerk-in-training, sprayed a man on the street corner with slush, threw a banana muffin at another driver who'd cut him off in traffic. The list went on. It filled two messy pages, front and back. Barkley feared his therapist would have him make amends for each tantrum, an idea he likened to the premise of a shoddy sitcom.

He anticipated they would read his tantrum diary together, and thus he needed copies. On the day it was due, he rode the elevator down to his condo management office only to find the door locked and the receptionist outside smoking a cigarette.

"Hey, secretary," said Barkley, peeking his head outside. "I need in the office."

"She's busy," said a maintenance man. He wore navy blue coveralls with the sleeves rolled back, and he was lean and wispy, with veiny forearms and tattoos up to his wrists. He and the receptionist had been arguing, and she appeared to be crying.

"I didn't ask you," said Barkley. "I said I need in the office, not my toilet's plugged."

"The fuck does that mean?" said the man. "Who are you?"

"I'm Frank Barkley. I own half this building." It was an egregious lie, and the man seemed unimpressed. "Wanna bet your paycheck on it, you prick?"

The receptionist flipped her cigarette into a snowbank. "Go to hell, both of you," she said, stomping into the building. Barkley gave a finger to the maintenance man and followed her inside.

She unlocked the office door, slapped on the lights, and threw her coat on a chair. She was tall and severe, bold like a fish hawk, and her cheeks had turned red from the cold. She slammed the phone back on the hook, then met Barkley with a mean look. *What?* said her expression. "I need copies," he said, floating his tantrum diary onto the desk.

"Copies," said the receptionist. "You got your panties stuck up your ass over *copies?*"

"No, I got my panties stuck … I am upset because it's working hours and the office was closed."

"It's noon, moron. I was upstairs making lunch for my family."

"No, you were outside hot-boxing cigarettes with that scum janitor."

"'Scum janitor,'" she said, giving Barkley the jerk-off wave. "You don't know anything. If you're so smart, you woulda looked at the sign and seen we're closed over lunch."

"Oh, I saw the sign," he said. "This sign?" He went to the office door, where a white placard was suction-cupped against the glass. It said WE WILL RETURN AT and had two dials connected to a clock face. "This goddamn sign says you won't return until six-thirty."

"I know that, dumbass. Give it to me." She took the sign and flicked the dials, which spun around and fell to the six position. She did it again, and again they fell straight down. "It's broken, what do you expect?"

Barkley took the sign back. He turned it over and spun the nut, but its threads were stripped. He pinched it, jiggled it, tried ripping the sign, and when it wouldn't rip he flung it like a frisbee against the wall, where it left a gash in the mauve paint.

"Jeepers," said the woman. "I'll make these copies now."

"I don't care if your family eats glass for lunch."

She disappeared into the next room with his tantrum diary. The copier whined to a start, and the woman kicked it or punched it, rattled a tray. When she returned, she tossed the papers on the desk and said, "Fifty cents."

"Suck ass, fifty cents!"

"They're double sided. That counts as two!"

"Come on!" said Barkley. "Do you have change for a dollar? Aw, fuck it."

He snatched his papers and turned for the door.

"My husband doesn't want another kid, and I do," said the woman. "That's what we were fighting about, if you're curious. I'm thirty-six. I don't have forever. I'll quit smoking. He can get another job." Her voice gave out and she wiped her nose with the back of her hand. "What do you care? You're just some dickhead making copies."

"I'm forty-three," Barkley said. "I don't have kids or a job."

"Then you don't understand. Leave me alone."

That afternoon he submitted the tantrum diary to his therapist. She assessed it with the indifference of a tract found on a bus seat. The diary was for him, she said, not her. She tore it into halves and more halves and dropped the scraps into the garbage.

"Are you fuckin' kidding?" said Barkley. "Here, I made a copy." She took it from him and discarded it in the same way. "Goddamnit, Doctor Olmedo. Are you trying to piss me off?"

She tapped a pen against her chin. "On second thought, you should have torn it up yourself," she said. "Oh well. Please do not look at me like that, Frank. Please, less intensity."

§

Later that week Freddi emailed the team. She said that with five losses and no wins, and only two games left, the Icekateers were easily the league's cellar-dwellers. But that was only if you gave a shit, which she didn't, so whatever. Still, maybe they should *try* to be decent? She proposed a team practice next Sunday morning.

Barkley read her email at his kitchen counter, sports talk radio in the background. It was late afternoon and he was eating a bowl of Choco Nugs. He replied all:

> whats up broomers. great part about the cellar is your always
> going down haha. even if the scores dont show it weve shown
> everyone we are the icekateers are a group of badass mother

He stopped. Would it be *motherfuckers* or *muthafuckas*? He poured himself more cereal, deleted it all, and adopted a more discreet tone.

> Dear Teammates, even if the scores haven't gone our way,
> we've put up a good fight. If we practice even once we can
> make a game plan to really strike some fear into our opponents'
> hearts. You bet your fucking ass I'll be there Sunday. We'll win
> a game, Freddi, and when we do instead of Gatorade we're
> dousing you with hot coffee.

He read the message back to himself. He changed *fucking ass* to *bottom dollar* and added a winking smiley. *All the beast,* he wrote for his closing, *Frank "The Ice King" Barkley.* As a postscript, he asked if anyone wanted to get a drink, typed his phone number, and he clicked send.

§

Sunday morning he got in an accident driving to the rink. A cold fog had dropped over the city, and he'd gotten lost. While he was parked against the curb studying the map on his phone, a truck fishtailed around the intersection behind him. Its tail end careened outward, snapping off Barkley's side-view mirror. The truck's brake lights flared up momentarily. Then it righted its course and continued down the street.

Barkley dropped his phone and laid on the accelerator. He was still in park, so the engine just revved. He shifted down and pursued the truck, beating his horn and flashing his high beams. Eventually the truck signaled right and pulled over.

"Hi there," said a man, climbing down onto the street. The man was about Barkley's age, wearing chinos and leather shoes. His truck, an old Bronco with a spare tire on the gate, belched out clouds of gray exhaust. "Some fog, huh? Did you order all this fog? Slick roads too. Black ice." The man put on a woolen beret with ear flaps. "Saw you flashing your lights. Everything all right, pal?"

Barkley punched him in the face. He grazed him, actually. His feet splayed out, and the man caught Barkley and held him upright.

"Slippery, isn't it? You're good, I got you." He steadied Barkley on the ice. "Boy oh boy, overtime at the fog factory today."

"Get your hands off me." Barkley shook loose and straightened his coat. "I'll smash your head through your fucking windshield."

"Ha—don't tell that to my wife," said the man. "She really likes this truck." Ahead in the Bronco, a woman craned her neck watching them. She wore big glasses and a stocking cap with a rainbow pompon. "Our kid's in the backseat."

"You be quiet," said Barkley. "Don't get close to me. I'll ram your goddamn truck into the river with your family inside."

"River's two miles that way. Are you lost?"

Barkley stepped back. He looked over at the broken mirror.

"Oh, I see," the man said. "Knew I'd come close. Yep, nuts."

"You could've killed me," Barkley said. "You weren't even going to stop. Plus, you're a little twerp with elephant ears and a pebble for an Adam's apple, and I want to knock your pissant face around just for that."

"Is this a gag?" said the man. "Quit joshing." He pulled off his mitten and grabbed Barkley's hand to shake. "I'm Doug Clancy. I'm the Clancy Man."

That didn't mean anything to Barkley. He yanked his hand away and assessed the mirror, which dangled from a black cable. Clancy poked at it, knocking loose a few shards of glass. "Uh-huh," he proclaimed, "busted." He kicked the ice from Barkley's wheel well, then crouched beside the exhaust pipe. "Smells like you're burning oil."

"Impossible. This car's not even a year old," Barkley said. "Get your insurance card."

"Hmm. We shouldn't rush to assign fault. You were parked an illegal distance from the curb."

"Don't dick me around, Clancy. My lights were on."

"Hey, what's this? This metal pole?" He pointed to Barkley's broomball stick in the backseat. "Golly, if you wanted me to crap you shoulda come out swinging that thing. Yikes."

They exchanged information. Clancy described himself as a struggling family man with sky-high insurance rates already, and he convinced Barkley to send him the bill directly. He scribbled his address on a worn receipt from his wallet, then folded it over. Barkley wrote his number on the back of an old business card from BuyAll.

"Pleasure meeting you, Frank," said Clancy, reading from the card. "Engine's burning oil. Probably need new wiper blades too." He winked. "All right then, happy trails." He whistled back to his truck.

Barkley thawed his fingers against the vents in his car. Ahead of him, Clancy said something that got his wife really laughing. She made a funny face into the backseat, then the brake lights flashed, and the Bronco pulled away.

Barkley set out for the rink. The next intersection was a one-way, and further down there was still no outlet. The street curved and he ended up on a frontage road, which led him back to where he'd started. He had another go and did the same thing. He reached for his phone and glimpsed Clancy's receipt. The ink was smeared and only his name was legible: *The Clancy Man*. And Barkley no longer cared about the rink. He didn't feel like practicing. This time leaving nothing to chance, he unlocked his phone and set the navigation for home.

2

That afternoon he lay under a blanket watching college basketball, an invitational tournament in Hawaii. Between commercials, the camera showed beachgoers on white sand wearing sunglasses and tiny floral suits. Barkley, unable to escape the chill of that morning, set the thermostat to eighty and wore his stocking cap. He made soup but wasn't hungry, brewed coffee but let it go cold. He scanned his email, but no messages arrived from the team. He fell asleep. He woke. The next game had begun on the television.

Stricken by an aimless, rabid urge, he paced his living room. He went outside and returned with a Sunday paper, but couldn't read beyond the first paragraph of any story. He cannot concentrate. His thoughts are restless and indistinct. He spirals down into panic.

He collapses to the floor, his body folding up into itself—knees against his chin, fists to his ears. His teeth clench and the wind escapes him. He is cold, sweating, but cold. A weight presses down from above: he undergoes a great compaction. He could suffocate in this manner, elbows smashed into his ribs. The carpet smells of feet, and the television plays brown noise. Something buzzes around his ears.

Barkley is not alone in the room: demons flank the corners, shadows surround him. The weight pushes further and soon he is writhing—a bullhead on concrete, a roach under a lens. He is pulled by wires and whipped with spurs, battered by stones, mocked by the demons. Unworthy of love, unfit for care. He feels worthless, helpless: he failed in going to the rink and was duped somehow by the Clancy Man. He is hopeless: he will never work again, he'll default on his mortgage, and soon he'll be on the streets in the cold. He is lonely and pinched with regret: no one can accept his nature, and he will live alone only to die alone.

In an instant he is drawn onto his knees. Just as quickly, he writhes out again. The shadow from above draws closer, it shrinks in toward him. An acidic foam rises in his throat.

And then it ends. He braces his arms against the sofa, regaining his breath as though he'd only just jogged a mile. His pulse recedes, his focus returns. The shadows scatter and the room empties. He goes into the kitchen for a glass of water, and as he reaches for the light dimmer, a bolt of static shoots from his finger and blows the fuse.

That night he cannot sleep. In his mind he diagrams a broomball rink: the red center line and faceoff circle, blue lines marking the zones, the goals and goal creases. He assigns his players their positions: a goalkeeper and two defenders, a half-back and center, two wingers. Then himself. Frank Barkley. He has no zone; he is drawn to the ball like iron to a magnet. He is stealth, he is elusive. His stick is a saber and his shots pierce like lasers.

An important match: he rallies his team in the arena tunnel. The lights blink out and the crowd goes silent, the air is pure electricity. Then Ted Nugent's guitar, the opening riff from "Stranglehold." The PA announcer growls Barkley's name, and the marquee flashes like a strobe. He enters the rink and takes a lap, salutes his fans and hoists his balls at the critics. And he and the team are huddled at center ice, pounding their brooms and chanting like warriors, when from his nightstand the phone rings and wakes him.

"Frank Barkley," says a voice. "You're in trouble."

"This is Frank. Hello?"

"I know it's you, Frank. I dialed your number."

Barkley sits up against the headboard. His alarm clock shows two in the morning. His legs are clammy and his mouth is dry. The phone says *Unavailable*. This is not a dream.

"Who is this?" Barkley says. "What do you want?"

"What do you want, Frank?"

"I don't know. I was sleeping."

"How can you sleep," says the voice, "with everything you've done?" It's a man's voice, leathery and calm, though it sounds far off like filtered through a tube. "I know all about you, Frank, and I want an apology."

"Go to hell."

"Right, that's the original Frank Barkley."

"Stop saying my name."

"Frank, I don't care if your heart catches fire and your chest explodes. All I want is an apology."

"For what?"

"That depends. How many people do you owe apologies?"

"I don't owe anyone shit."

"Right, you and your stupid swagger," says the voice. "You're a loudmouth."

"Shut up, asshole," says Barkley, kicking back his blankets. "You don't scare me. I'll stomp your throat for calling so late. Travis? T-Storm, this isn't funny."

"Who?"

"You, you dirty dog!"

"What?" says the voice, laughing. "You don't know me, Frank. You might as well be talking to yourself. Listen—"

"No," says Barkley. "You listen, tough guy. You don't know *me*, because if you did, you wouldn't threaten me. Keep laughing, dickhead, see what I'll do. I don't take shit! I'm the monster that sleeps under your bed, I guzzle gasoline and fart fire!" That was stupid. He should stop talking. "Stay on the line—I'm tracing this call. You better crawl into your cave, start praying. I'll call in the helicopters, I'll bring the dogs. I'm Frank fuckin' Barkley, you know it!"

There's laughter on the other line—enormous laughter. "Helicopters!

Holy shit!" The voice is muffled, as though it's laughing into a pillow, and when it strikes a fever pitch the call abruptly ends.

Barkley slams his phone on the nightstand. Its display casts the room with an eerie marine glow. He is wide awake, sitting against his headboard. His heart is racing, but he's not scared. He is sweating, and he's shaking, but he's not scared.

§

It cost $200 to have the side-view mirror fixed. At Barkley's request, the mechanic ran a diagnostic to check if the engine was burning oil. It wasn't. The mechanic said Barkley was crazy for thinking it would.

Back home, he searched online for Clancy's number, but he'd forgotten his first name. He searched "the Clancy Man" but got no results.

§

That night he scored again. Deep in the defenders' zone, Barkley dropped to one knee, swatted his stick like it was on a fulcrum, and punched an angry shot on goal. The ball lofted up and bounced past the goalkeeper, who swung belatedly with his hand and fell.

"Nice hit, Ice King!" Freddi called from center ice, clapping her pink gloves together. "Real pretty," said T-Storm, whipping Barkley's ass with his stick. "That's highlight material."

The Icekateers held the lead only a couple minutes. Their opponent was a group of pasty scrubs called the Mighty Sucks, who scored two quick goals on chance and clumsy defense.

Late in the game, an oafish man in a bicycle helmet swung high and struck Michelle in the back of the head. Michelle crumpled to the ice. Play halted. Freddi and Erica Lynn rushed over, but Michelle waved them off. "No, no, I'm fine," she said. "It just surprised me." She patted the bike-helmet guy on his shoulder, and the referee sent him to the box with a minor penalty.

"That careless piece of shit," T-Storm said. "I should kick that guy's ass."

"Power play!" Barkley said. "We can still win this."

After the drawback, the ball moved from Erica Lynn to Freddi, who fell just inside the defenders' zone. Barkley gained possession and scooped a pass to the point, where Bogey trapped the ball with his foot and lined up a shot. But then Darryl Drummond wandered in and collided with Bogey, they spun like lovers in a music box, and an opponent swooped in and cleared the ball down the rink.

"Drummond, you turd! And Bogey, you suck!"

Moments later, Barkley took a hope-and-prayer shot on goal from behind the center line. His shot was straight and true, yet it kept going, rising over the rink lights and clearing the chicken-wire backstop, landing far out of sight in the snowy field. Barkley stomped his boot, slipped, and fell. One of the Sucks tramped through the snow to retrieve the ball.

When play resumed, the bike-helmet guy climbed back over the penalty boards. T-Storm immediately cross-checked him, sending him sprawling forward on the ice. "High-sticking piece of shit," T-Storm yelled. "Hit a girl, you piece of shit."

The referee shrilled his whistle.

A Suck bum-rushed T-Storm but was blocked, diplomatically, by another teammate. T-Storm threw off his gloves to fight, but Freddi wrapped him up with both arms.

"Sit down, butthead."

"Fuck you," T-Storm shouted.

"Fuck yourself!" someone shouted back.

Freddi lost her balance and fell, bringing T-Storm down with her. Another Suck tripped over Erica Lynn's stick, and a woman charged at Erica Lynn. Bogey grabbed her elbow, but then he, too, slipped and fell. People wanted to fight, or else halt what might become a fight, yet no one could stand long enough to do anything meaningful. A Suck reached out to help Bogey, and Bogey pulled him down and punched him in the neck. The referee dove in to separate them.

"Grow up," said a female Suck.

"Grow tits," said T-Storm.

Barkley arrived late to the scene, having first been restrained by Darryl Drummond. His fury was vague and diffuse, and as a matter of convenience he lunged at the bike-helmet guy. "Agoobag," he yelled, or something unintelligible. The guy turned to Barkley, resting his stick over his shoulder like a hobo's bindle, and whacked him square in the face. Barkley fell to the ice. Just as quickly, he was back on his feet.

"Sorry," the guy said. "I didn't see you there."

"You son of a bitch," Barkley said. "That was a cheap shot."

"It was an accident. I didn't mean to." Then the guy did something for which Barkley was unprepared: he reached out with both arms and embraced him, a breath-clearing bear hug. "I'm sorry, galoot." The guy's beard was rough and bristly, and he smelled of sweat and cheap musk. Barkley was disgusted, yet he couldn't manage a thing to say. He patted the guy's back.

"Cut the grab-ass," T-Storm called from the penalty box. "You'll make me puke."

Barkley subbed out, leaving the team short-handed. His temple throbbed where he took the hit, tender to the touch. He already knew it would become a black eye. What was his plan jumping into the fight? He had no plan, and if he hadn't been blindsided, who knows what he might have done. Nothing smart, that's for sure.

After the final whistle, both teams shook hands at center ice. T-Storm and the bike-helmet guy exchanged words of apology. Freddi reminded everyone about the final game next week. No one mentioned anything about yesterday's practice. Barkley suspected no one else showed up either.

§

His phone rings at one in the morning.

"Frank," says the voice, "you're awake."

"You again. Thanks for calling back, asshole, you owe me two hundred bucks. I'm a lawyer, Clancy. I will hunt you down and collect, with interest. You and your family. And I don't need new wiper blades either. Hello?"

"You're talkative tonight," says the voice.

"I had a broomball game. I can't sleep." Barkley sniffs back a runny nose, still cold from the bitter night air. "Is this the Clancy Man? In the Ford Bronco?"

"Maybe."

"Is it someone from BuyAll?"

"I could be anyone, Frank. Maybe I'm your conscience."

"Sure, that makes sense. Go choke on your own dick." He pulls the cord on his nightstand lamp, but it's too bright, and he extinguishes it. "What did I do to you, huh? Give me a hint."

"*Me*? It's not just me, Frank."

"Then what is it? Why are you calling?"

"I want to hear you say you're sorry."

"But I don't know what I did," Barkley says. "You could be anyone. I've done bad things, and I made a lot of people mad."

"And do you wonder, maybe, if that's why I'm calling?"

§

February closes out with record lows. Northern winds sweep down, turning everything brittle and rigid. In the streets, bodies are indistinguishable in their parkas and scarves, cars are uniformly gritty with salt and sand. The sun warms nothing, only casting the downtown grid in odd, transient shadows.

The calls continue. The voice persists.

Barkley cancels the weekly session with his therapist, thinking she might be cranking him as part of his treatment. Then he decides against it, reschedules, and openly cries to her for the first time.

"The days are so long," he says, "yet they add up so fast. Every night it's like someone's standing on my chest. I could die tomorrow and leave nothing behind, *nothing*. It's too much pressure. I'm responsible for my own life, but holy shit." He is grinding his teeth and squeezing his fists. "God, I hate my ex-wife," he roars. "You know, I'm in my forties and I can't even grow a beard. My clothes are *ugly*. My career is gonna be toasting bagels and serving coffee out a window to twerps. Oh, and guess what. The Vikings' kicker still sucks, the Wild are pathetic, and the Timberwolves blow ass! Goddamnit, I can't catch a break!"

"What are you not telling me?"

"I think I'm hearing voices, Doctor Olmedo."

"Hmm," she says, but shakes her head. "No, that does not happen to you. You are not the type."

§

Freddi emails the team, saying those with new jobs should call in sick Tuesday: after the final game, they will be drinking. The forecast predicts bone-numbing cold, so plan for bourbon shots lit on fire: blazing saddles, hot tamales, Kentucky fireballs, flaming assholes.

§

"Why do you answer, if you don't want to talk to me?"

"Because I won't back down. I won't run away, and I won't quit."

"That's some attitude, Frank. And how's it working out for you?"

"I get by."

"Sure you do," says the voice. "What's the black eye from?"

Barkley brings a hand to his face. By now the bruise has faded into a marigold crescent, still puffy and soft. Clancy couldn't know about the black eye, nor would anyone from BuyAll. It's two in the morning and Barkley is in his living room. The lights are off and he's on the sofa, swaddled in a blanket.

"Don't you want these calls to end?"

"But how?" he says.

"I told you already. You need to apologize."

Barkley gets up and looks out the window. Red lights blink atop all the downtown buildings, and a single limousine glides down the street. The sidewalks are empty. No one's outside. It's too cold for that.

"Sorry," he says.

"Oh, no, I want a better apology than that. I want you to mean it."

"Sorry for what, then?"

"Take your pick," says the voice. "Do you really need me to tell you? You kicked a taxi in a crosswalk, how's that? You spit at a bum on Nicollet Mall. Threw a muffin in traffic. You flamed your old boss online—is this familiar? Frank, is this familiar?"

"Sort of."

"You cursed a woman for throwing cellophane in the street. You dinged someone's car because they were double-parked. Chucked your remote when the cable was down. Yelled at your condo receptionist and made her cry. You shout on the phone, and you're a bully in public. You're not much for sportsmanship either."

"You're right," says Barkley. "Go on."

He knows who's calling him. These were entries from his tantrum diary—all except the fight with his receptionist. When he'd gone to add that one, the pages were already full, margin to margin. As the voice continues, he goes to his desk for his housing association binder.

"You butted into a man collecting signatures. You never hold the elevator. Here, you yanked a kid's earbuds on the bus because his music was too loud. Why were you even riding the bus with your temper?"

Barkley is in the stairwell now, where his phone cuts out and the voice comes and goes. "You hurt people, Frank … you bulldoze them … get what's coming … have no family … did these things, Frank … can't take them back!"

"I'm sorry," he says, back in another hallway several floors below. "I really am. When you say it like that, yes, I can act so poorly."

"And why are you sorry?"

"Because I would do it all differently, if I could," he says. "Every single time, if I'd only stop for a second and think, I'd do it differently. Truly, I'm sorry."

"And like that," says the voice. "You are forgiven."

"But I wasn't asking for your forgiveness."

"We're done now, Frank. Goodbye."

The call has ended. The hallway is silent. Barkley knocks softly on the maintenance man's door, knowing there's a child inside. When no one answers, he knocks again.

The light in the peephole goes dark. Barkley puts his face to the door and speaks.

"I was already sorry," he says. "And I'm already filled with remorse. So what good was this little exercise? Because I'm still here, and you only made me more angry. Don't pester me anymore, okay? Stupid in the first place. Don't call me again, because you can't tell me anything new. I already know my faults and failures, I live with them every day. And I am sorry. I'm not just saying that. I didn't mean to make your wife cry. But if you want me to change, don't provoke me. I'm trying to do better, but I'm doing it my way."

He steps back from the door. He can't tell anything from the peephole. And he could stand here all night, torn between the urges to offer a truce or to shove the man over his balcony railing. He looks at his phone, but it's not ringing. He scans the hallway, and he's alone. So he walks away, his heart like a distant drum in a vast and foreign field, and back upstairs he gets into bed, and soon he is asleep.

§

The final game of the season: the coldest night yet, the air thin and penetrating.

The Icekateers win control on the drop, until Michelle promptly falls and turns it over. Their opponents attempt a perimeter pass, then they too turn it over. Erica Lynn fumbles her stick and whacks T-Storm in the shin. Darryl Drummond is absent on defense, wiping his nose with a dish rag. Barkley watches for a while from the penalty box. Bogey falls into an opponent, who falls into Freddi. The match continues like this, errant passes and wayward shots, pileups and breakdowns, no strategy and even less skill.

Late in the second half, the game still tied at zero, Barkley slides into a scrum behind his own goal and emerges with the ball. He turns up the rink, where a dusting of snow provides him traction along the boards. When an opponent tries screening him, he passes ahead to himself and shoulder-checks the man. When another opponent crouches low on defense, Barkley fakes a pass to Bogey across the wing. Ahead, the ice is free and clear. He angles in toward the crease, and the goalie steps backward into the net. "Fuckin' do it, Ice King!" he hears from behind.

Barkley has a move. He is prepared for this moment. The move is classic misdirection, a deke to clear the goalie. It works like this: he sweeps the ball outward and dives onto his stomach, and as he slides forward, he hand-passes across his own body. The goalie lurches into the post. She falls. The net is wide open. Barkley engages the ball with his stick—all it will take is a nudge. But now he has a different idea. He cocks back and goes for the kill.

He whiffs.

His head strikes something, the goalpost. His trajectory changes, and he collides into the boards. Things are blurry. Somewhere off and away he sees the orange ball, not in the goal.

No one is cheering.

And Barkley is no longer thinking about broomball. His thoughts have moved on entirely. He's no longer there in the rink, piled against the boards on his stomach. Could it be he's nowhere—an absence, devoid of light and vacant of sound? Or that he's somewhere—a deep well in which he falls slowly enough to admire the masonry, a glass elevator rising into the clouds? His worries and dread have left him. Barkley is untroubled. His mind is empty, he's at peace. Though he's not dead, of course. It's just an injury, probably a concussion.

"Ha! Your head sounded hollow. I heard it from the other end." T-Storm yanks on Barkley's sleeve and pant leg, turning him onto his back. "Come on, asshole. Time's almost up. You didn't score, but we all had a good laugh."

"What an absolute boner," Freddi says, shaking her head. She squats onto her haunches. "Wait, he might be hurt. We shouldn't move him."

"No, he's fine. Look at how he's clutching his stick."

"But his eyes. He looks bonkers."

"That's normal." T-Storm nudges Barkley with his foot. "Let's go. Get up, Ice King. You okay?"

He's okay. He'll get up in a minute. Don't worry, he's fine. He wants to keep playing. He wants to be so good that while everyone else plods and shuffles along the ice, it's like he alone is dashing through a field of thick summer grass. He's getting up. He's fine. He wants to win.

(THE ANCHORING ROOT)

You can walk in one strict direction and arrive at a place called nowhere. You'll know it by the open air and leveled earth, the sense of unthreatening monotony. Everything stretches here—the sky, the fields, the days. Cornstalks splinter underfoot, and dust swirls your hair. The sun might tucker you, the wind lull you, yet you'll seek neither shade nor shelter. Far out will be jackrabbits and coyotes, rumors of a mountain lion. You'll give them hardly a thought. Instead, you'll remember hearing of a laborer shot through the foot with a nail gun, how vines curled up his legs and roots secured him to the soil. His wounds clotted with sap. The sun blistered his lips into bark. The wind blew through him and he waved his branches, shedding parts of himself, and thus was birthed a new civilization. For their totem was chosen a plain metal stake. That was one ending; the other was that he calmly waited for his leg to rot.

CHARGES

I used to live a fast life. Not a *big* life, but a busier one. I worked a research job in the city and shared a warehouse loft with my then-girlfriend. I was a serious person, wearing tan pants and subscribing to two different newspapers. Then something might have fizzled inside my head. I'm not being scientific here. But life got complicated, and I was harangued by weird feelings of guilt. I saw hopelessness in the shadows between buildings, hatred clouding up from snarls of traffic. I was attuned to the ills of man and sensed myself gravely complicit. Everywhere I heard voices—not made-up ones, but didacts on the radio, commuters on their phones, arguments from the loft next door. One night I blacked out—not even drinking; I just plain blacked out— and found myself walking the median between lanes of the interstate without shoes. All it took was that one time, and I knew I had to be different.

I moved back to Apex, my hometown, and claimed my parents' basement. I was thirty years old, feeling I'd failed at adulthood and it was no one's fault but my own. Then a house came up on short sale, a flimsy stack of rotwood just down the street from my parents. I bought it. I changed my diet, kicked the caffeine, the nicotine, ditched my TV at the Goodwill. I started a lawn care business and attempted a life that might keep me, if not happy, occupied.

§

One afternoon my truck slammed a pothole on the county highway, launching the weed whacker from my mower trailer. As I was kneeling on the shoulder inspecting the damage, someone yelled at me from a speeding blue Toyota. I looked up just as a paper cup smashed across my face, drenching me in root beer and rolling me backward into the ditch.

Ahead, the Toyota braked in the middle of the road. Two teenagers peeked at me over their seatbacks. Their names were Darold and Samantha, as I would later learn. I leaped up and chased after them, but they peeled out and soon disappeared over a slope.

That night Gary Munsen called me at home. Gary is a burly lunkhead who acts as sheriff. Earlier that day, he and his rube intern, Dougie, had seen me at the diner in Circle City. Given that I was covered in dirt, grass clippings, and brown syrup, Dougie teased that I'd allowed someone to crap all over me. "Positive ID on the Root Beer Bandits," Gary said over the phone. Darold was Dougie's younger brother, and Samantha was Darold's halfway-girlfriend. "Smoking gun? The blue Toyota. Ain't many blue Toyotas around here. Most everyone in this county drives a pickup truck."

"That's fine," I said, "but I've already put the root beer thing behind me. You can tell the kids I wasn't injured. It was probably my fault anyway."

Gary sighed into the phone. He said that without my charges of assault, Darold and Samantha were mere litterbugs. Littering is the least of offenses, hardly worth the paperwork it entails. "But me and Dougie got an idea," Gary said. "Tell me about this business of yours. What's this truck you're driving?"

I do lawn services, I told him. Epic Lawn Care. I'll do it all—mowing, weeding, aerating, timber clearing, tilling. It was my first summer in business. I'd adorned my truck and trailer with custom decals, which showed my name, number, and a cartoonish figure of me: wiry limbs and wide smile, ponytail flowing out the back of my cap, gloved hands clutching a rake face and leaf blower like they were shield and saber. The caricature ran both sides of the cab, step rails to roof. It was silly, but it was promotion. I wanted to work.

Gary's idea was for the kids to shadow me for a day. They would atone for the root beer, plus they'd see how a grown-up, meaning me, makes his living. I'd get free labor on the deal. But make no mistake, it was community service. I was to put the kids to work.

"Oh," I said. "Sure. Okay."

"Okay? You're agreeable. I was gonna bribe you."

"No, I could use the help," I said. "And sometimes I get lonely."

"Hmm." Gary made a spitting noise, chewing tobacco. "Well, good you agreed. This was actually Dougie's idea, so whatever."

"Whatever sounds good to me," I said. "It could be interesting."

"And I should say, Darold's mom was concerned you'll be a pederast, or one of them guys who wears other people's skin. I said you're more the type to get lost watching the clouds and ram your truck into a school bus."

"I'm none of those things," I said. "But thanks for sticking up for me, Gary."

§

The next morning I woke with the sun, put on work jeans and a clean t-shirt, steeped herbal tea in my thermos, and took the long way to Circle City to meet Darold and Samantha.

Circle City is one of the county's lesser towns. Its one diner is also its one gas station, video store, and nail salon. I'd already finished my tea when the two kids finally stumbled half-asleep up one of the town's few roads.

They were both about sixteen. Darold had a fullback's build: short and blocky, thick-shouldered, square-jawed. He looked like a kid who had entered puberty early and then stalled. Below his chin floated a dusty, unformed goatee. Samantha was long and sharp limbed, a good six inches taller than Darold. She was an Oyate Indian girl, the outdoor type, manic and untiring. And she liked talking.

"Good morning, mister," she said, climbing into the cab. "I'm the one who hit you with the pop. In the face, right? *Whoosh!* I didn't mean to, at least not in the face. He dared me. I said no. But then I was like, root beer sucks. Did it hurt? Did you cry? If you cried, I'm sorry."

"Put on your seatbelts, please," I said.

"No, seatbelts wrinkle your clothes," Samantha said.

"That's not true," I said. "Besides, I'm told this is meant as a learning experience. Please listen to what I say."

"Fine, geez, you don't have to yell at us."

"I wasn't yelling," I said. "My voice is perfectly calm."

We left Circle City on the highway back to Apex. Darold slumped against the passenger door, and Samantha sat between us. We ran a line between corn and soybean, weedy pasture, stock ponds where cattle slopped in the morning sun.

"Where are we going?" Darold asked.

"We're going to work, Darold. We have a full day planned."

He wore a Detroit Tigers cap with a flat brim, which he tugged over his eyes and tried going to sleep. Samantha plucked off his cap and put it on her own head. "Why are you called Epic Lawn Care?"

"Because no job is too small, Samantha."

"Then shouldn't it be Miniature Lawn Care?"

"No job is too big either."

"Oh, fascinating. Am I sitting on something? What the …?" She unearthed a rock-solid bottle of wood glue from the crack of the bench seat. "Nice truck. Maybe it could be louder. Why don't you drive a diesel, since you're hauling this trailer?"

"Actually, I ran a cost analysis of diesel fuel versus unleaded—"

"What's this button do?"

"My yellow flashers." I flipped them back off. "I know what you're thinking, and they're not sirens. They mean, 'Look at me and please don't run me over.'"

"Can we turn on the air conditioner?" she said. "It's literally a million degrees."

"I like the sensation of wind rushing through the open windows."

"Dougie was right, you are a space case. Do you have a wife? Or are you one of those guys who pastes magazine pictures of ladies inside your closet door?"

"No. And no. And the air conditioner's broken."

"Why don't you cut your hair? Are you poor? My family's poor too."

"That's enough questions, Samantha."

"Did you fart? Did *you* fart? Do you care if I fart?" Et cetera.

§

We came to a vacant lot not far outside Apex. "Here we are," I said, nosing up against the highway so my truck could be seen from either direction. "Up and at 'em, Darold." From the utility box I got some hedge shears for Darold and a pair of gardening gloves for Samantha. "Get the big stuff around the edges," I told them.

"Edges of what?" said Darold. The place I'd pulled into was just a big borderless area. In my youth it had been a Tire Hut, but the building had now been razed, its foundation sunken beneath the far-off weeds. "Look at us," he said. "We're already at the edge of the world."

"We need to unload this mower. Darold, see those metal clasps? Lift up on the tongue and we'll release these straps."

"You can call him D-Bag," Samantha said. "How come I got gloves? I'm just gonna … pull things?"

"Don't call me D-Bag," Darold told me. "She's playing."

I released the mower straps myself. I pulled down the ramp landings and aligned them with the mower wheels. "Are you watching, Darold? You'll be doing this by lunchtime."

"I'm gonna cut your hair with this big scissors."

"Are you talking to him or me?" Samantha said. "Maybe you can scrape that little caterpillar off your chin."

We got to work. I mowed while the kids threw weeds at each other. Shortly I idled up beside them. I directed Darold thirty yards downroad, where he could trim away the milkweed below a pizza billboard. Samantha I told to yank some purplish weeds and pile them beside my trailer. A semi-truck rolled past drifting the odor of cattle.

After the lot, I mowed the ditch. This never fails to delight me. Those tall, thick weeds smell good when they're cut. Samantha yelled what I think was a question, but my cushioned ear mufflers reduced it to static. I smiled and launched her an A-OK sign.

Darold was chasing a wasp with the shears, which seemed a reliable way to impale oneself. In turn, I chased Darold with the mower, tooting the little horn behind him. "Gimme," I mouthed, collecting his shears. I rumbled over to the truck and returned with three rakes. We gathered the clippings into three separate piles, though I'll admit there was no reason for doing so.

"Do you have any water?" Samantha asked, returning me her gloves.

"Or beer?" said Darold. His shirt was too long, almost down to his knees, and darkened with sweat.

"Yeah, he's gonna give us beer. Plus, it's ten in the morning. Drink this," Samantha said, "whatever's in this jug."

"Not that," I said. "That's Round-Up."

"Oh yum, Darold, like 7 Up."

"Har dee har. Look, I made you this," he said, unrolling a six-foot-long papery breadstick. Behind him, a large gap of plywood showed through on the billboard.

I sorted things back into the utility box. A Silverado pickup drove past and barked its horn, to which Darold hurled up two middle fingers. Samantha flipped his Tigers cap into the air, trying to land it on her head.

"Hey, what's your take for this job—" Darold asked, "like, fifty bucks? I think me and Sammi deserve ten each."

"That's not the system," I said. "You're getting something better: on-the-job training." They stared at me dumbly. "No, I'm not getting fifty bucks."

"Forty," Samantha asked. "Thirty?"

"I'm not getting thirty either. I'm not actually …" I thought of how I might phrase this. Our work was an investment, I said. We weren't making money—not directly. Soon I would make money, once I booked some real jobs. "Today you might call pro bono."

"He means charity," Samantha explained.

"Not charity," I said. "Publicity." I indicated my truck, the big decals, my likeness, my phone number. And I told them what I'd been doing all summer: "I drive around and park in high-traffic places, trying to be seen." No one had hired me yet. I'd loitered in Apex, Circle City, every jerkwater town and township in the county. People here take pride in their own yard work, I'd been learning.

I said, "I'm faking it. I don't know what I'm doing."

"You're mowing weeds. Darold is pouting. I'm looking good."

"You're thirsty," I said. "We'll go to my house and you can drink from the hose."

"The hose," Samantha said. "Are we *dogs*? Do I have fur and big droopy ears? Are these fleas? Did Darold sniff your crotch first thing this morning?"

§

Instead, I gave them each a bottle of water from the cooler in my truck bed. We drove around Apex, the county seat. Apex is the highest spot for miles, a former military outlook against Indian uprisings. Now it's just a town with a quarry and a grain elevator, decrepit office buildings, streets without curbs, lawns without sidewalks. I found myself sullen, as if speaking my situation aloud had made its hopelessness all the more real.

This happens sometimes: I fall into patterns of silence. It happened a lot in the big city. Desperation would get the best of me, or discontent. I'd clam up beyond rescue, and in recognizing my moodiness only bury myself deeper in it. My co-workers would avoid me, suspecting I was constipated; or my girlfriend would apologize, thinking she had somehow wronged me. But that was never the case. When I would tease out my silence, I'd find the true culprit was my own private shame, a cunning thing because its source was so often inane or idiotic: regret from eating too much licorice, bitterness over washing tissues in my jeans, childishness from still confusing my cardinal directions. My self-criticism bled into self-pity, the ugliest posture a man can adopt and admittedly the hardest to break.

"Enough already," Samantha said. "Can't we listen to something else? What is this?"

I dug around the door panel for the case to *The Cosmos and You*. Samantha took it and puckered her face. "It's a cassette tape," I said. "I got it for a quarter at the library surplus sale." I pulled a wrinkled paperback off the dash. "This too, which I actually think is a load of hooey."

"*Dianetics*," she read. "You don't need to lose weight."

Darold snatched away the cassette case. He ogled it, shrugged, returned it. "I thought it was a little video game," he said.

"How would this be a video game," Samantha said. "It's just a plastic box thing."

"Look at the picture. That eagle's standing on a comet. And dolphins wear sunglasses?"

"Does mister look like the sort of guy who plays video games? Maybe tiny train villages, or something."

"Tiny train … what? No. What? I like music," I said. "I like the Grateful Dead."

"The who?"

"Yeah, they're good. *Quadrophenia*'s killer. I have it on vinyl."

"Words, please."

I said, "Years ago I had this old tour shirt from when the Dead played Egypt in '78. I got it from an auction site on the internet. The shirt was cream colored, and the silk-screening was flawless. Thing was, I never wore it for fear I'd spill pasta sauce or tear it on a nail. So I boxed it up in my closet, and eventually my girlfriend threw it out. But I couldn't get angry, because I should have treasured the shirt while I had it. See the lesson?"

Samantha offered me the book and tape case like they were radioactive. "We've drove past Sticky's ten times already," she said. "Are we ever gonna eat lunch? I'm so hungry I could eat a cow's butt."

"That's what steak is," Darold said. "Unless you meant a cow's butthole. Which is gross. I like rap," he added. "And country."

"Those are two things I hate," Samantha said. "Three, if you count cow's butthole."

I pulled into the gravel lot for Sticky's, a salt-and-butter pit where varsity jocks binge on carbs and construction men curse through mouthfuls of starch. "You two go ahead," I told the kids. "I have lunch in the cooler. Tomato sandwich and carrot sticks."

"That's not lunch," Darold said. "That's rabbit food. Come on, Peter Cottontail."

As we were walking in, Samantha said, "You're more fun when you're talking, even if it is nonsense. And who throws out someone else's t-shirt? *Not* your fault."

§

I ordered fruit salad, Darold a bacon burger, Samantha two caramel rolls. Our waitress, a buxom, bucktoothed girl not long out of high school, had refilled Darold's Pepsi three times before she finally brought our food. We ate. Darold and Samantha sat across from me, brushing knees and pinching thighs beneath the table. Elsewhere, men in crusty lime-green shirts flung back their chairs, belched, and scattered coinage for tips.

Darold's phone rang. "Yo, talk!" he said through a mouthful of fries. "Eating. Sticky's. We *were* working. I don't know, weeds and stuff, plants. He's here. Guess. You are what you eat—he ha! Yep." He handed me the phone. "Dougie."

"Hello, Dougie?" I said.

"This is Gary," said a voice on the other end. "I'm on Dougie's phone. Why don't you have a cell?"

I excused myself into the video casino. Gary and I talked. He wanted to know if the kids were behaving and that I was keeping them busy. Watch my gas cans, he said, Darold was known to huff. I wasn't letting them toy with my saws and hatchets, was I? If Darold slept, I could slap him. If Samantha chattered, I could send her to the truck bed. I had permission to run them, berate them, force them into calisthenics. That seemed unnecessary, I told Gary. Everything was wonderful. No hassles. Easy wind, peace in the valley.

I returned to see Samantha with a handful of our waitress's hair, pumping it like a well handle. "You got a dirty mouth," she yelled, spraying a bottle of blue fluid in the waitress's face. "We're gonna clean you up, greaseball!" The waitress writhed away, bumped a table and spilled a pitcher of water onto the floor. Samantha swept her leg and kicked a shin. She pounced, locking the waitress in a half-nelson.

"Whoa, whoa!" I shouted. "What's this?"

"It's a fight, dummy," said Darold.

I went to pull the girls apart. I ratcheted Samantha's waist and hauled her away, but my grip failed. I stumbled into a table, knocking two road workers from their chairs, bowls of chili crashing down beside them.

"Drown, bike stealer!" The waitress flung a cup of bean soup at Samantha, missing widely. It splattered against the front window of the restaurant. The girls circled like pugilists in a ring, then Samantha sprung forward, thrashing her arms windmill-fashion. She and the waitress shoved one another, slapped, spat, flailed their limbs.

Darold, transfixed, dumped his Pepsi on the floor to no good cause.

From the kitchen rushed a man in shirtsleeves and a tie, a paunchy bald guy with smeared glasses. He pinned back the waitress's elbows, restraining her. I was on my feet now, bear-hugging Samantha.

"She called me torpedo tits," the waitress said.

"Dumb Indian?" Samantha loosed an arm and patted her mouth in a war call. "Scalper?"

"Both of you, break it up!" said the guy in shirtsleeves, the manager. "Becky, kitchen! Now! Red Thunder, out!"

The waitress shucked him and lunged forward, but I'd turned away Samantha, and the waitress smashed her nose against my shoulder. She recoiled, moaning. The manager wrangled her to the kitchen. Darold hooked Samantha's elbow and tugged her to the door.

"Where were you?" I said.

"Are you kidding?" Darold said. "Stop *that*?"

I helped up the road workers and straightened the tables, made apologies profusely. The dining area was like the set of a gross-out game show. I wiped the front window and mopped the floor with napkins, only spreading the mess. "Hey," said one of the road workers, "it's that lady from the side of the truck." The manager came and I paid our bill, both of us staring into the counter. When I turned to leave, he said, "Wait, take these." He handed me three plastic containers from a display case, each holding a slice of chocolate pie. "Sorry," he mumbled.

"I'm sorry," I echoed. "I feel like this is my fault."

§

"Did he give you pie?" Samantha asked. "Old Button-Down. He's a pie pusher. We do that sometimes. Why the look, mister?" We were heading east out of Apex, past the highway department and the fertilizer plant. "I do hate that girl. We call her Becky Breastfeeder. She had tits in fifth grade and a kid sophomore year. No one likes her."

"Guys like her," Darold corrected.

"Did you steal her bike?" I said. "Whatever, I don't wanna know. You can't go around confronting people like that."

"Oh please, mister. Contrary to popular opinion, not everything's my fault." She braced her hands against the dash. "Leadfoot, are we on the lam?"

I looked down and saw I was doing eighty-five. The engine was clanging like an old boiler. I eased the pedal and took a deep breath.

"Gary and Dougie said you should be paying us," Darold claimed.

We left Apex on the highway behind us. The road flattened out between electrical pylons and brown pasture. "Don't go this way," Samantha said. "Anywhere but Circle City." I turned onto a rutted gravel road which crossed a few culverts, trailer homes sinking down into the soil, wild turkeys, odd varmints.

"We should be working," I said. "Working calms me down. We'll go to Brownville. We can clean some lots, trim branches. We'll put your energy toward something productive."

"Nah, let's go somewhere there's air conditioning," Darold said. "I'm pitting out like swamp thing. Let's go to your house."

I considered this prospect. The scene played out before me, those two balking at my lawn-chair-and-card-table furnishings. The summer heat had curled my yellowish wallpaper. Cluster flies had swarmed the windowsills, and I'd taken to sucking them up with a vacuum hose. Darold would wrinkle his nose at my earth-toned tie-dye tapestry. Samantha would open my fridge and find it empty. We would flag, surly, saddled with lethargy. Time passed as I was thinking this, enough that my silence alone stanched Darold's suggestion.

Samantha said, "No offense, mister, but I thought you were gonna teach us things."

"I can try. I'll tell you how to build a latticework screen … how you stack a retaining wall … how to flush voles from your yard …"

The kids showed no interest. We hit a two-lane blacktop and zipped through Brownville, which is easy if you blink. Brownville's a dumpy little burg, though lately I'd pruned around some outbuildings and mowed the ditches. Now, I'd venture to say, it was only a couple coats of paint short of a place you might take pride in.

"Tell me, then, what *do* you care about?" I said. "What do you two want?"

"Get rich," Darold answered. "Big money shot caller."

"That's the stupidest thing to want," I said. "But maybe it will make you happy, I don't know."

"I want to be a college basketball player," Samantha said. "And then an Olympics basketball player. We'll fly to Greece and play people who don't even speak English, and I'll dunk all over their faces. Folks in Circle City will name the town gym the Sammi Red Thunder Arena, and I'll go, '*Guys*, you didn't have to do that!' Then I'll be a coach, and I'll wear nice suits, and I'll weave gold ribbons in my braids so no one forgets."

"I'll buy you gold medals," Darold told her. "I'm gonna be a record producer. Gold chains, gold teeth, big golden chalice," he said. "Look out: squirrel party."

I slowed. Up ahead, a group of squirrels was scavenging corn that had fallen off a harvest truck. I honked and they craned their necks, then scurried off into the ditch.

"Just because you wear baggy pants doesn't make you a record producer," Samantha said. "You probably have to go to school. And you can't sleep every day until noon."

"Don't hate," Darold said. "I want it more than anything. So it will be."

"Come on, doofus," I yelled. "That's not how the world works! You don't get what you want just because you want it. It takes effort, and discipline, and even then it takes luck."

Darold's jaw slacked. "What's doofus?" Samantha wagged her head, rolled her eyes. She said, "Then what do you want, mister?"

"*Jobs*," I said. "I like working! It gives me purpose. My days have structure when I'm working." My knuckles had gone white around the steering wheel. "I want a tornado. It can shred people's yards, thrash their trees, and I'll be busy for months."

That was the right answer. Samantha pumped her fist while Darold bared his teeth in a vicious, depraved way. I got the idea they liked destruction.

We reached the county line. I pulled into a farmer's approach, backed out, and turned around. The squirrels had cleared the road by our return. We kept on, slowly, in no great rush. "The joke goes like this," Samantha said. "Why don't you hit an Indian on a bike? It's probably your bike." She air-drummed a rimshot. "Now why do people hate Becky Breastfeeder?"

§

All this happened in August, a month that stores the worst of its heat for late afternoon. That's when the sun creeps away and the light angles fiercely downward. It's the time of day, I imagine, when cats purr contentedly in sunbeams, and when office workers trudge to vending machines for cans of diet pop. It can be treacherous driving west with a dirty windshield, oppressive going east into your long, incessant shadow.

The three of us hit a period of silence. Darold's chin pinged against his chest, and Samantha began to sigh unknowingly. In the previous hours we'd done no work. Instead, we batted rocks into fields using broken fence posts, sat in the shade below billboards and played gin rummy.

I turned onto a county road that looped north of Apex, not wanting to drive through there again. When the trailer rattled behind us, Samantha shot to attention. "No," she commanded. "Not this way, mister."

"I'm taking you home," I said. "We've done all we can today, which isn't much."

"The lookout tower—did I say that? Or was I thinking it?" She tugged her cheeks with both hands, facing me with a ghoulish look. "I said we're going to the lookout tower."

"I heard you," said Darold, "but maybe I was dreaming." He lifted his cap and scratched his blond, pointy hair. "Sometimes I feel like this is all a dream. Like we're only puppets, and the string guy is seizing up." Although I considered Darold a minor numbskull, I'd had this thought myself. It came when I acted in ways I couldn't explain, when my impulses were clear but my motives anything but.

"The tower's closed," I said. "Why would we go there?"

"To work," Samantha said, "which in your case means being seen."

The tower marks the tallest point in Apex. It's three open-air platforms made of rotten fir wood, stacked with rickety slat scaffolds. "It's closed for a reason," I said. "Do you know the history? The tower was like a citadel on the prairie. Army guys used to monitor the Indians from there. Then it became a tourist attraction, then it got shut down. It was falling apart, and civil right groups didn't want it as a reminder," I said. "Put on your seatbelts."

"We can sit around, or we can work," Samantha said. "We *would* work, if you asked."

"When I was in high school, we carved our initials in the tower. Seatbelts. That's part of why they closed it off. Kids would go there to break bottles and make out."

"Still do," Darold said.

"People say that's where Becky Breastfeeder got pregnant. Like you could really know that," Samantha said. "Oh, mister, look where we are. They should call this spot Root Beer Falls, because you got—" I whomped my passenger-side tire over the same pothole as yesterday, vaulting the kids from their seats and ramming their crowns into the ceiling of the cab. They dropped in a heap on the bench seat. "Mister," Samantha yelled, "you did that on purpose!"

"Oops," I said, "my mistake."

Darold clucked, jutting his jaw out and back like a bantam rooster. "I might've swallowed my brain there. Is that a thing? Go back, let's do that again."

§

At the bottom of Tower Hill was a slumping cattle gate with no lock. Darold jumped out and kicked it open, and I drove through. The road switchbacked through trees and dirt cliffs, ending at a gravel lot bushy with dandelions. Sedge populated the hill, and wildgrass sprouted along a ring of orange snow fencing, which encircled the base of the tower.

I parked far off in the lot. "Not here," said Darold. "No one can see us."

"Good," I said. "We're not supposed to be here."

"Publicity, dum-dum." He snapped on my yellow flashers. "Here's the most visible place in the county."

I pulled onto the grass, angled the truck so you could see it from my house and my parents' house, Sticky's, the quarry and grain elevators, the downtown office block—and, this being a clear day, Circle City, Brownville, and beyond.

The kids stepped over the fencing and went for the tower.

"No," I shouted after them. "If people can see us, they'll see us working."

I gave Darold the weed whacker, bent and scratched but still operable. He didn't know how to use it, but whacking weeds isn't exactly skilled labor, and I taught him in only fifteen seconds. Samantha I gave the cordless hedge trimmer. It's sharp, I told her, so hold it out away from you. "My body is not a tree. Got it, mister." Darold by then was hoisting my chainsaw, laughing in a terrifically maniacal way. "Let's start small," I told him, lowering the chainsaw back to its case. "This you graduate up to."

We worked. I helmed the mower, Darold buzzed around the gravel lot, Samantha sheared clusters of knapweed. The kids weren't doing precise or even necessary work, but they at least seemed enthused. Breeze cooled our sweat and pollen caught the sunlight. We stayed busy. There was nothing magical or mystical about it, except that this area was lush and overgrown, so the work went slowly. That's how I like it. Slowly is my way now.

Then we were done. Or we ran out of useful work. The kids ran up the tower, and I grabbed the pie from the cooler and joined them. Up on the topmost platform, we tested the boards, then sat and hung our legs over the ledge. Out ahead of us was all of Apex, its derelict buildings and rundown roads. I was glad for the distance. The air seemed cooler up here, fresher, thick with the clean, musky scent of pine.

"Uh-oh," I said. "This graffiti, it says, 'D-Bag eats assholes.'"

"Yeah, I wrote that about Dougie," said Darold. "But then people started calling me D-Bag too. Backfire."

"Hey, I had this thought earlier," Samantha said. "You can't eat a butthole. It's just a hole. It has no mass. Am I right, mister?"

I did not deign to respond. Out ahead, birch trees cast long, spindly shadows, and bugs swarmed over stagnant puddles. To Samantha, I said, "I'm sorry for what Becky the waitress called you. That was cruel."

"Why are you apologizing? You didn't say it."

"No, but I feel responsible in some way."

"Well, do me a favor," she said. "Next time you're at Sticky's, punch Becky in the mouth for me."

She studied her pie. We had no forks, so she delicately scooped its graham cracker crust. As it reached her mouth, a piece broke off and dropped mousse onto the crotch of her pants. "Damnit!" she said. Darold laughed, until he dropped his pie in a similar fashion.

"Double damnit," he said. I pressed up my container from the bottom and managed an easy bite. The kids raked pie into their faces, slurped mousse off their fingers.

Because I was shielding my eyes from the sun, Samantha nestled Darold's baseball cap on my head. "Gross—" I shook it off. "It's all sweaty." The cap bounded off the platform and floated to the ground. "Oh, I'm sorry, Darold."

"Dude," he said, "shut up with the apologies."

"Wait, do you hear that?" said Samantha. "There's another car out there."

"Oh, great." Darold nodded to where the sheriff's SUV had begun its winding ascent up the hill. "Here come Gary Gunslinger and Deputy D-Bag. They're gonna yell at us."

The SUV stopped on the gravel below us. Gary's scanner barked, and Dougie pointed ahead at Darold's cap. They kept sitting there, no idea we were watching them from fifty feet above.

"Check this out," I said.

"Don't do it, mister. He's gonna hawk a loogie."

"No," I said. "Watch." And I heaved my pie like a shot put, launched it down at them, blooming their windshield in a perfect brown smudge.

MAKE IT YOURS

Maguire starts telling a story to the men in the truck. The story is about an old concrete worker named LaPointe. It's raining outside, and that's why the men are in the truck. They are concrete workers themselves, state employees who attend to highway bridges.

LaPointe was an Oglala Sioux who'd been full-time with Maguire seven or eight years earlier. One morning they were on a bridge down by Castlewood, where a berm had cracked and diverted rainfall out over the soil embankment. Over time, the rainfall had washed out a gully large enough for a man to lie down in and go to sleep, if he so wanted.

The berm was a simple repair. Maguire and LaPointe knocked out the bad concrete with a jackhammer, drilled anchors and built a plywood form, mixed two bags of quick-setting concrete and shaped the new berm with trowels. To fill the gully, Maguire took the truck and drove back to the county shop for asphalt millings.

But it started raining on the drive—it started pouring. Maguire knew the rain would compromise the new berm, and it would clog up the air compressor and jackhammers, which they'd left sitting on the highway. These were only minor problems, as Maguire explains to the men in the truck. He and LaPointe could fix the berm later, and the tools would dry out. But then Maguire got to thinking about LaPointe alone back there in the rain. He turned around in a farmer's approach and returned to the bridge.

Let me guess, interrupts Barnett. You had a tarp for the air compressor. And you found the Indian hiding beneath the tarp.

Barnett is the other full-timer. He sits shotgun spitting sunflower shells into a Styrofoam cup. In the back seat are the two seasonal employees, Dunn and Jim Gates. Dunn, now in his third summer on the bridge crew, has a newspaper folded to the crossword puzzle on his lap. Jim Gates, who is only eighteen and new to the job, leans forward to hear Maguire through the patter of the rain. The men are on a two-lane bridge over the narrow James River, hemmed in by orange traffic barrels.

He wasn't under the tarp, Maguire says. Dunn, you got a guess?

Climbed down the embankment and took cover under the bridge.

You boys lack imagination, Maguire says. And I guess you never knew LaPointe.

To know LaPointe was to know the state's laziest worker. Yet LaPointe wasn't dumb. He knew the berm hadn't cured, and it would wash out before the storm even passed, pissing away his and Maguire's work. They'd need to come back tomorrow, hammer out the bad concrete, and start again from scratch.

So LaPointe worked out a solution. He draped his windbreaker over the berm and sat his ass in the gutter of the bridge deck, deflecting the runoff to a drainage grate. When Maguire returned, LaPointe was reclining in his underwear, exposed to the rain, his arms stretched out against the guardrail.

Once the storm passed, Maguire climbed down from the truck. LaPointe stood, undid his ponytail, and wrung out his hair. They lifted the windbreaker to find the new berm dry as a drought, perfectly formed. A grain truck idled over the bridge, its driver gaping at Maguire and the half-naked Indian.

LaPointe's clothes are heaped on the ground, Maguire says. His boots, jeans, shirt—soaked. And he goes, 'Maguire, you didn't get the asphalt millings. Now what are we gonna do?' And I say finding him dry clothes might be the more pressing matter. 'You're right, I can't work like this,' he says. 'Go get the millings, and I'll lay low while my clothes dry out in the sun.' Which was his scheme all along, just his trick to get me on the shovel.

Barnett chuckles from his seat up front. Dunn pencils in a few squares on his crossword. It's still raining, and out beyond the bridge, a crow swoops crookedly to a fence post, catches an odd gust, and flies off again.

Jim Gates asks, So what. Was the Indian okay?

Was LaPointe okay? Maguire says. Couldn't have been better. If he got sick and missed a couple days of work, he was all the happier for it. Hell, LaPointe would just as soon do a rain dance if it meant we could sit our asses all day in the truck.

§

Weeks later the men have moved west to the bridges over Snake Creek. It's late June, hot and dry, and the men's arms have browned and their lime-green shirts have bleached in the sun.

The bridges here suffer a number of small structural problems. One day the men might swap out plywood spacers between guardrails, and the next they might drill drainage holes through the concrete decks. On one occasion they use an air compressor to blow out sparrow nests from the steel support beams. Most often, though, they repair spalled concrete. Bridges grow weak by delamination, which is when water seeps through the concrete and rusts out the steel rebar. To repair it, the men set signs and block off traffic, hammer out the chips and flakes, sandblast the rust, then pour new concrete directly into the roadbed.

They are not a hard-working crew. They take breaks often. Each morning around ten, they lay down their tools and Barnett will sit on the tailgate and smoke, while Dunn will nap or read the paper in the truck. On one morning in particular, Maguire retrieves a bottle of water, and he and Jim Gates lean against the guardrail over the creek. Out in a pasture are forty cattle all wearing yellow tags in their ears. The breeze carries a scent of earth and manure.

Maguire begins another story about LaPointe.

It's a long story, he says to Jim. Me and LaPointe were best friends—you get that way when you're on the road forty hours a week with someone. But he was an odd one, Maguire says. I can't say I ever understood the man.

LaPointe had no car, so Maguire would pick him up on the highway each morning, then drop him off there again each night. This was near Groton, a one-stoplight town, where LaPointe lived with his brother, his brother's wife, and their two daughters. They were a hard-luck family—fights, illness, debt. Maguire recalls stories of unpaid bills and burnt food, threats and indolence. LaPointe didn't drink, and he was the only one in the family who worked. Some nights he wasn't safe at home, and he would escape by walking the streets alone after dark.

Groton, at night, might as well board up its windows and declare itself a ghost town, LaPointe had once said. He might pass a choir recital or a Legion baseball game, but otherwise the town was just a public pool and a rusted-out playground, a few dirty bars and a four-lane bowling alley. Trucks sat cooling in their driveways, and woodsmoke drifted on the air. At night LaPointe would cross every street and avenue, coasting like a wagon down a gentle slope, meditative and empty of thought. And then one night he came to attention to see a married couple through the picture window of their living room.

The couple was a woman and man, perhaps in their thirties. She stood against a wall dancing—or so it seemed—sweeping her hands like she was tying knots on an imaginary board. Though the woman appeared pale and underfed, her face and arms glowed with freckles. The husband sat on a recliner, wearing a baseball cap even though they were indoors. At intervals he mimicked the woman's gestures, repeating them or adding his own.

Probably sign language, says Jim Gates.

No shit it was sign language, Maguire says. He leans over the guardrail and spits down into the creek. Any idiot could tell it was sign language.

The woman was the deaf one: she was more articulate, more precise. She might hook two fingers like links in a chain, brush her palm like a pendulum, spin her fist as if she was reeling in a fishing line. And though her signals meant nothing to LaPointe, it hardly mattered what she was saying. Her hands moved with rhythm and grace, harmony, choreography.

And then the woman looked out, and maybe she was startled by the Indian in the street, or maybe she only saw her own reflection, and she came to the window and closed the drapes.

LaPointe returned to the house. He made a habit of it. Soon he was watching from the corner of the couple's yard, within the branches of an old-growth blackjack pine. The tree smelled of Christmas, and its bark scattered the ground like a jigsaw puzzle. One night a teenage girl walked past with her golden retriever, and when the dog didn't so much as sniff in LaPointe's direction, he knew in that tree he was as good as invisible.

The couple didn't always converse. Some nights he might be lucky to even glimpse the woman crossing the window. Or the man might sit in his recliner, listening to the television and stitching leather at a small wooden table. Sometimes the drapes would remain shut the entire night. Other windows would light up and go dark—the kitchen, the bedroom, a mud room or a laundry room. When this happened, LaPointe would sit within the tree, eating pretzels and smoking Newports, attempting stories through gestures he invented on his own.

But when the woman signed, these were the nights that kept LaPointe in the tree. Watching her, he felt his worries flee and his fears melt away. It wasn't sexual attraction. Instead, he felt a sense of communion, a sense of oneness, as though she revealed her spirit in the rush of her hands, the roll of her shoulders, the focus in her eyes. Even without understanding the woman, LaPointe found he could anticipate her next movement.

After a few weeks, he told Maguire about the deaf house. They were between bridges in the truck, and LaPointe described first seeing the couple from the street, the elegance of the woman's gestures, the young girl and her dog, the relief he felt having a place of his own. He promised Maguire he meant no harm. And then he explained what he'd seen the night before.

The couple had been arguing—shouting, as LaPointe described it, signing more fiercely and more urgently. The woman made a gesture like a knife being twisted, then she stormed away. The garage door opened and she stepped onto the lawn. She wore a sleeveless blouse and crossed her arms for warmth, looked up at the cloudless, starry sky. She stood not twenty feet from LaPointe, and in the moonlight he could make out the constellation of her freckles.

Then the man appeared in the driveway. Though her back was turned, he began to speak. He was sorry, he said, he was slime, he was dirt. He said he wanted more in life and felt trapped, and he wanted her, his wife, to have more as well. They deserved more. They deserved better. *She* deserved more—more security, more opportunity, more happiness every day. The woman turned, and upon seeing her husband flinched. He made three careful motions: an extended pinky, a thumb to his lips, a fist on his chest. *I am sorry*, LaPointe knew.

Sorry for what? asks Jim Gates.

Maguire drinks the last of his water and pitches the bottle down into the creek. The sun is bright, blinding even, and he shields his eyes to look out into the pasture. He takes his leather gloves from his back pocket, calls for Barnett and Dunn, and the men go back to work.

§

After Labor Day the region shop hosted its annual surplus auction, where it sold skid steer attachments and bales of wire, power tools and hand tools, bulky metal desks, phone systems and the like. Along with the paint and sign crews, Maguire and LaPointe took down bids and moved equipment when it came off the auction block. Not everything sold. The leftover items were dumped on a flatbed trailer bound for the Salvation Army, and from that pile LaPointe plucked off an old cream-colored electric typewriter.

Maguire tells this part of the story weeks after the men have moved on from the Snake Creek bridges. By now they're on the interstate, where the traffic is faster and more frequent. One day recently, Jim Gates nearly stepped into an open lane and had his cap blown off by a passing semi-trailer.

Maguire tells the story in fragments, an incident here and another there. He doesn't bother with it when Barnett and Dunn are around. They'd never understand, he tells Jim Gates.

LaPointe's typewriter was in a sorry state. It rattled like a diesel engine and blotched most of the letters. After the auction, the seasonals were cut and the full-timers lingered around waiting for plow season. On these days, LaPointe retreated to the machine shop, where he hunched over a workbench repairing the typewriter.

The work was tedious and on a miniature scale. He unscrewed the faceplate and pried off the letter faces, soaking them in gasoline to remove the gunk. He blew out the interior with an air compressor, then scoured it with solvent and a wire brush. To silence the rattling, he busted off toothpick ends, which served like tiny shims, between the harness brackets and carriage. And as final steps, he scrubbed the exterior with hot soapy water and polished the wood inlay with linseed oil. One afternoon he unveiled the typewriter to Maguire.

And it was good as new—*better*, Maguire says. But so what? Still a goddamn old worthless typewriter. I tell LaPointe he'll be lucky to get ten bucks for it, and he goes he's not trying to sell it. 'It ain't for me, Maguire,' he says.

LaPointe wrapped the typewriter in green tarpaulin and took it home to Groton. At this point of the story, Maguire is forced to speculate. His guess, he says, is that LaPointe took it straight to the pine tree—why else would he cover it with the tarp? But it being an electric typewriter, it was no more useful unplugged than a rock.

So it was for the deaf woman, says Jim.

Or her husband, Maguire says. Or both. I don't know that LaPointe had much of a plan.

A week passes before Maguire resumes the story. The men move to another bridge, which crosses an old rail line overgrown with purple aster. It's mid-summer and hasn't rained in weeks. Dust and pollen whirl in the air, coating the men like ghosts.

So I ask LaPointe about the typewriter, Maguire says one morning by the supply trailer. He's been all sullen since taking it from the shop, but he needs to talk, I can tell.

LaPointe wanted to give the typewriter to the deaf woman and her husband. His rationale was simple: it would fill the gaps in their communication. One night after the house went dark, he left it outside their garage door, only to find it the next night moved to the curb like a piece of garbage. Again he set it outside their garage, again finding it moved to the curb.

So he sits tight with it, Maguire says. But he *needs* to get that typewriter in the couple's hands. 'They'll know what to do with it,' he says. 'Trust me.' I tell you, Gates, he was obsessed. You'd say his name five times before he'd hear you. He'd meet me on the highway with pine needles in his hair and sap on his sweatshirt.

LaPointe had to get closer—and his purpose had to be clearer. He stole an ink ribbon and a ream of paper from the supply closet at work. Back at his own house, he typed a short, anonymous note explaining the gift. That night at the tree, he set the typewriter in a wicker basket he'd snatched off someone's porch. He was going to leave it on the couple's front steps, ring the doorbell and hurry away, then leave the woman and her husband alone for good.

§

That August, Jim Gates takes his turn with LaPointe's story. One Saturday he and his girlfriend, Marcy May, take a green Wenonah canoe out on the Elm, a narrow, winding river colored brown with the sediment of farm runoff. Jim starts with the scene of LaPointe waking before the deaf house as if from a dream. He explains LaPointe's joy in watching the woman sign so fluently. And to absolve LaPointe, Jim claims he'd fallen into the tree on accident, and that he'd never meant to intrude on the couple's privacy.

Marcy May is a stern young woman. She wears thick glasses with flip-up shades, and leaves no skin exposed for fear of sunburn. When Jim narrates the girl and her golden retriever walking past the tree, Marcy May interrupts him. It doesn't seem like that could happen, she says. Didn't you say he was smoking cigarettes? People would smell that.

But the tree was really wide, Jim says. Think of it like a canopy tent. Or like a fortress, even. When Marcy May shakes her head, he says, I'm just telling you what Maguire told me.

Well, who told Maguire?

LaPointe did.

So LaPointe tells Maguire, Maguire tells you, and now you're telling me. Don't you think somewhere along the line things could get confused?

Get confused? Jim says. No. You don't know Maguire, okay? He's got no reason to lie.

Marcy May allows him to continue. He tells the story up to LaPointe waiting with the basket in the tree. But then he stalls. He doesn't know what comes next, he has a feeling it's not happy, and he sweeps his oar in the water and they continue down the river. Their canoe passes by pylons and electrical wires, which crackle like a bug zapper in high heat.

§

By harvest the men have gone north again, up to the James River bridges where they'd started the summer. The work, which had never seemed urgent, seems even less so now. The men sweep gravel off the bridge deck and seal expansion joints with caulk, simple jobs that don't even require closing a lane of traffic. In a down moment, Jim Gates asks Barnett why LaPointe quit the bridge crew.

LaPointe … *quit?* Barnett says. He didn't quit. Do you mean …?

Did he get fired? Jim asks.

He didn't get fired. You don't know the story, do you? Barnett says. LaPointe's dead.

What? Jim asks. How?

Barnett lifts his shirt and wipes the sweat from his chin. His stomach is loose and as white as kitchen flour. I don't know why Maguire keeps telling this story, he says. He'll never get inside that Indian's head.

Yet Jim doesn't press the issue. He waits on Maguire, but Maguire keeps his silence. It's almost Labor Day, and as a seasonal employee Jim will soon be cut loose. Late one afternoon, when they're together in the crew cab, he asks Maguire to finish the story.

Didn't I finish it already? Maguire says. What was the last part?

LaPointe's in the tree with the basket. He typed a note for the couple. So what happens next?

Maguire rolls down his window and lets in the air. They're passing through a small glacial valley, pasture for cattle, swampy water at the side of the road. So LaPointe's in the tree, Maguire says. The drapes are pulled open. It's dark out, and he's waiting for his chance.

The couple had been arguing again, but now they were ignoring each other. The husband worked at his small wooden table, and the woman walked by without stopping to signal a word. When she'd leave, the man would shout at her—LaPointe could hear his voice, garbled. Finally the man got up from his recliner, and in this moment LaPointe went for the door.

Now on the front step, he could see to the other side of the room. The man had pinned the woman against the wall with his forearm. He was stuffing a scrap of leather into her mouth. The woman squirmed, clutching her hands around his throat. And then, all at once, the man let go and she dropped to her knees. He leaned over and tried signaling, but she punched up and struck him in the chest. He fell backward onto the carpet. The woman stood and brushed her hands, while he crawled alone back to the recliner.

A cattle truck passes in the other lane, its trailer scattering mud and straw.

And? Jim says.

And LaPointe ditched the basket in the tree and went home, Maguire says. The end. It might still be there today, who knows.

Bullshit, Jim says. He didn't leave the typewriter in the tree. LaPointe wouldn't do that.

Says who? What do you know about LaPointe?

Tell me the truth.

The couple moved away, Maguire says. And LaPointe moved away too. For all I know, he's back in Pine Ridge. You lose friends when you're an adult, Gates. Me and LaPointe don't talk anymore.

Barnett told me LaPointe died.

Barnett doesn't know shit, Maguire says. Barnett didn't drive ten thousand miles one summer with LaPointe. And neither did you, Gates. You never heard LaPointe's stories about his menace brother and his drunk sister-in-law and their two helpless kids. You didn't watch him lose thirty pounds in a single month because he couldn't eat, he was so caught up trying to help that deaf woman and her husband. It's not your story, Gates. You can't choose how it ends.

Jim turns away and looks out the window. He's crying but he won't let Maguire see. I don't know what to believe, he says.

Believe what you want. I'm telling you LaPointe gave up and went home.

§

This much is certain: LaPointe died later on at the deaf house. I knew he would die seven years ago, when I first tried telling this story. It had to be tragic, I believed. I was younger then, more cynical, and I couldn't imagine LaPointe's meddling going unpunished.

But the story was complicated in my mind, and I could never get it right. Details about sign language, the mechanics of concrete repair, the creeks and fields and bridges of northeastern South Dakota—they diverted my attention from the characters of "Make It Yours." For a long time I studied a book I found online, Edgar D. Lawrence's *Sign Language Made Simple*. Once, on a Saturday in October, my brother-in-law and I scouted the James, Elm, and Maple Rivers, taking more than 200 photographs of the landscape and the undercarriages of bridges. And I even worked two summers on a bridge crew myself, breathing in concrete dust and sweating through my jeans, trying to imagine the world as LaPointe, Maguire, and Jim Gates might inhabit it.

In the last seven years, I've tried telling this story from each of their perspectives, and each man's story was different from the next. For a while Jim's father, a newspaper journalist, had a role. There was a time when Jim and Marcy May put down a blanket and made love in the shade beside the Elm River. One night I had Maguire shoot fireworks at a highway patrolman while hiding in a salvage yard, and another night he watched the lights in his ex-wife's farmhouse through field binoculars. As for LaPointe, I forced him to loiter outside the bars and bowling alley in Groton, hoping someone would invite him in for a drink, though no one ever did. And one time he took his nieces into the tree, where they both fell asleep, and he carried them home in the first snow of the season. These details seemed unimportant, but you can believe them if you like.

Through every iteration, I couldn't imagine LaPointe living to the end. He was always going to die. And for the longest time, he died violently. The deaf woman's husband, to me, was the wild card—a vicious, erratic man. But when he spoke his long apology that night in the driveway, he became more than the simple terror I'd planned him to be.

So here, in the end, is how LaPointe dies. Time and again, as he tells Maguire, he tries leaving the typewriter outside the deaf house. You can imagine how the couple thinks it's junk, and how LaPointe's message is lost. Everything Maguire tells Jim Gates is true, even the man strangling his wife with a piece of leather. That fight, however, happened weeks earlier, one of many LaPointe witnessed and described in the truck.

On the night LaPointe dies, the house is in fact quiet. By now he's abandoned his idea to leave the basket on the steps. He's decided he needs to get it inside the house.

Before doing so, he lugs the typewriter to the town park, plugs it into an outlet at the pool shelter, and composes a new letter. He explains how he's watched the couple from the blackjack pine and the anguish he feels—deep down, in his true heart of hearts—over their failure to connect. The typewriter, he says, is a small gift, which they can use sparingly when signing isn't enough. And he returns to the house, late, once the windows are dark, jimmies the lock on the garage, and goes inside.

The drapes are open, and moonlight paints the corners of the living room. The air is salty like beef broth or stew. LaPointe sets the basket on the wooden table and rolls his note into the paper feeder of the typewriter. Then he turns to leave and sees the woman in a doorway behind him.

Who are you? she says. Her voice is round and inarticulate, unpracticed. She speaks from her diaphragm, a deep, guttural sound. I live here, she says.

LaPointe indicates the typewriter in the basket. He points to it and then to himself, and he shapes his hands into a heart and holds them over his chest.

Leave, the woman says.

Read the note, LaPointe whispers. He takes her by the hand and guides her to the typewriter.

The woman screams—loudly, deeply, a tortured moan. She plows into LaPointe and knocks him on his heels, and he stumbles backward, cracking his head on the corner of the table. It could be that his neck snaps, or his skull fractures, and he falls in a heap on the carpet.

The husband rushes in from their bedroom. His wife, by then, has slunk down against the wall. He crouches beside her and grips her shoulders. What happened? he says. What is it? And it takes several attempts before she can explain it with her hands. The husband checks LaPointe's breath. There is blood in the carpet. He and his wife don't see LaPointe's letter—not yet—but it becomes, in time, the most legible part of a tragedy that bonds them.

(GOLDEN HEART PARADE)

There's a latitude where even whiskey freezes, where bolts snap like chalk and you chop your water from the creek with an axe. Up here, the light is gray and paltry when there's light at all. No roads or radio, no one watching for flares. You wend your way among the spruce, tread upon flat, unbroken snow. The wind becomes your symphony, the stars your endless theater. Little to do but secure shelter, conserve energy—control what you can, which is only your breath. You might even think you're the first in all of history to walk this land, but that's false. Men have died here before you; they'll die here after. Take the prospector who discovers a vein of pristine ore, only to mark his claim and stumble backward down a mine shaft. Or the Sherpa who in a blizzard walks circles, always tripping over the bodies of his expedition party. The naturalist among black bears, his final field entry observing a rise in aggression. These men were mavericks, pioneers, renegades. Their legends outlast their names. They died from hubris or distraction, or maybe nothing more than rotten luck. These, too, are natural causes.

BEACON LIGHT

At age fourteen Rachel Dahl got in bad with a boy. The boy's name was Brad Van Laecken. He was three years older, but he wasn't in school.

One weekend Brad and his uncle had a poolside room in the large atrium of a hotel. Rachel was there for a friend's birthday party. All afternoon the friend's dad had been keeping watch on Brad and his uncle, who were sitting at a patio table drinking out of plastic cups. They'd been keeping to themselves, but anyone could tell their thoughts. The birthday girl, she was now thirteen. She and her friends were all wearing two-piece suits. Finally her dad approached Brad and his uncle and asked them to leave.

"Excuse me," said the uncle, spitting out a wafer of ice. "You want us to leave? And why's that?"

"To be honest, you're making me nervous," said the friend's dad.

This was February in Duluth. One wall of the atrium was all windows. It wasn't yet five o'clock, but already it was dark out.

"I don't believe you're within your rights," said the uncle. "We're paying guests at this hotel. You're just a guy in tan pants and leather shoes."

The friend's dad turned to see the girls as Brad and his uncle saw them, in the shallow end of the pool, some floating on curved foam noodles, others playing keep-away with an inflatable ball. The girls were bright and lively, untiring, but they were *girls*—pale skin and braces, doughy arms, high-pitched voices clanging off the surface of the water. Only Rachel Dahl was outside the group. She sat dangling her legs in the Jacuzzi, wet hair like palm fronds matting her neck and shoulders. Water roiled from the jets and steamed up the air around her.

2

The next Fourth of July, Rachel lay on a blanket by Lake Superior with her friend Helen Voight. It was dusk at Canal Park and the food vendors were out along the boardwalk. In the air was a drifting haze— the Kiwanis Club had been handing out sparklers.

Someone stood over Rachel's blanket. "I know you," said a boy in black jeans and a sleeveless shirt. "Holiday Inn. Remember me?" Rachel looked to Helen Voight, who shook her head. "It was someone's birthday," said the boy. "You remember."

"No," Rachel said, "you're thinking of someone else."

"You had on a polka-dot top. Your hair was longer then, and blonde."

"Ugh, go away, would you?" said Helen Voight. She flitted her hand like he was no more than a mosquito. "How gross," she said once he'd left.

The fireworks began over the water, launched from a barge a few hundred yards offshore. They started slowly, with blue and red blasts. The theme that year was Philly Freedom, and at one point the rockets formed a golden Liberty Bell, crack and everything. Shells exploded like beats on a steel drum. Sparks surged outward and lit the sky so brightly it seemed like the middle of the day.

Afterward there was applause, and a tinny version of "This Land Is Your Land" played from speakers by a bandshell. Rachel rolled her blanket, and she and Helen went to where their bikes were chained against a large black statue of a nautical anchor. "Don't look now, but he's standing by his car," Helen said. "Out on the street—don't look."

The car was a Ford Mustang, one of the boxy, ugly-year models. It was lit from above in a halo of streetlight, its driver-side door open and the boy resting his arms over the frame. Rachel began walking her bike over.

"Wrong way," Helen said. "Rachel ... *Rachel!* All right, bye. Rachel, call me, will you?"

Slow Down Boy

Brad was neither charming nor witty, but he was tall and his arms were tan. He complimented Rachel's eyeliner and asked what all her bracelets meant, and he said the two of them ought to drive up north and watch the rich folks' fireworks. That was more commitment than Rachel wanted, though. She told Brad to keep talking. He recalled seeing her by the hotel pool—Super Bowl weekend, he said. His uncle had won $200 in roulette, and they'd rented a room with a big-screen TV and split a jug of scotch. Brad said he remembered Rachel by the Jacuzzi, the way she appeared alluring and untouchable and only half-formed through the steam.

She let Brad finger her in an alley behind the bakery. His method was sudden and violent—all prodding, no rubbing. Rachel made sounds like she thought would be expected. They quit when a garbage lid clattered on the pavement—a stray cat, probably, or a raccoon. Rachel buttoned her shorts and climbed onto her bike. When Brad said to call him, she said she didn't know his number.

"Call me at work. Two one eight—"

"I didn't say I want your number," she said, pedaling away with the blanket weaved around her handlebars. "Maybe I'll see you, maybe I won't. So long."

4

Though she did see him again. That summer she saw him driving past her team's softball practice with his arm out the window, and then she saw him drive back the other way. She saw him in the neon lights outside the Banana Split, eating fries slathered in ketchup. And one night when she was biking past the lake, she saw him sitting on a bench, alone and staring out at the timber cargos, as if that was a perfectly natural thing to do.

Rachel had no one to tell about Brad. She and her friends had split up in the manner of teenage girls, and her three older sisters were out of the house. Her dad had long since moved out, and her mother sometimes stayed in bed or went mute for days. It was that summer Rachel first felt the dark, nagging feeling—that she was alone in the world, no one to confide in and only herself to trust.

Take Me Away

Shortly before Labor Day she biked to the Cattle Corral and took a stool at the bar. "I want a Manhattan, please, and after that a gin fizz," she said. She tried seeing back into the kitchen. The Corral was a homestyle restaurant made to look like an old barn, its walls hung with leather bridles and boot spurs and antique branding irons. Rachel had seen Brad's car outside and knew he was a line cook there. "Is Brad working?" she asked.

The bartender, a brunette woman with braided pigtails and painted-on freckles, filled a glass with ice and poured something clear and bubbly from a hose. "Who?" she asked. *Brad*, Rachel said—dark hair, crooked nose, scruffy face. *Brad*, drives the Mustang. "Oh, him," said the bartender. "I don't know. Brad? I can go see."

"Tell him his girlfriend's at the bar. Hey—" said Rachel, taking a drink through her straw. "This is just Sprite."

For the next hour she watched a baseball game and played photo hunt on a tabletop video machine. She drank two more Sprites. The bartender brought her a plate of chicken fingers and said, "From the kitchen. The guy wants me to say his shift's almost up. Listen," she said. "You look like a nice girl, okay? It's already late. I'll put this food in a box, and I can say you got a call and couldn't stay. Do you understand?"

"Thanks, but I'm not as young as I look," Rachel said.

She and Brad parked behind the fertilizer plant, where the lamps were all busted and weeds grew from the flaking concrete as wide and tall as garden shrubs. Rachel turned in her seat and said, "Can I talk to you?" School was starting next week, she said. This would be her first year at the senior high. She didn't like who she was, and she was afraid of being picked on, or getting lost, or being trampled in a crowd. All her sisters had run cross-country, she said, and she thought maybe she could do the same.

Brad didn't seem to be listening. He chose something heavy and industrial from his CD booklet, then he leaned across the center console and put his tongue in Rachel's mouth.

Everything was awkward in the front seats. Brad's skin was oily and his hair smelled like the fryer vats. He put his arms up Rachel's shirt and tried unclasping her bra, then he reached up and twisted the skin of her neck between his fingernails. She pulled his arms down and moved away. "Will you take me back now?" she said. "I just remembered I have something to do in the morning."

Brad wiped his mouth with the back of his hand. "I didn't hurt you," he said. "That's how you like it, anyway. You want it to hurt."

"No," Rachel said. "I don't."

6

That fall Rachel joined the cross-country team. She started the season on junior varsity, but by the fourth meet she outdueled a sophomore girl and got promoted. Rachel's role was that of supernova: she would charge out at the start of each race, wasting herself in an attempt to wear down the opposing schools' runners. Then at the third mile her three fastest teammates, all seniors, would overtake the pack and sprint home. At most meets the seniors finished one-two-three, and soon Rachel was placing in the top ten herself.

A boy named Darren Hunt took a liking to Rachel. Darren was stringy and long-limbed, his complexion the color of paste. Although he was only an eighth-grader, he'd been elected junior varsity captain, and sometimes he sang the stretching cadence and called on Rachel to join in harmony. *Dollface*, he called her. It embarrassed her to no end. Still, she went with Darren once to a movie and another time to the homecoming football game, but nothing clicked between them. While Rachel appreciated Darren Hunt, she found him too safe and far too devoted.

The region meet was held that October on a golf course overlooking Lake Superior. At the second mile marker, Rachel saw Darren running past the coaches and spectators, cheering her on. The course looped around a small pond and then crossed over to an adjacent fairway, where he reappeared loping through the rough grass. Although the other runners were at her heels, Rachel flashed him a discreet wave. Then Brad Van Laecken emerged from the trees, thrust out an arm, and clotheslined Darren Hunt, who wasn't even facing forward, and Darren's feet went out and he skidded to the ground.

Rachel blinked hard and shook her head, all in stride. And suddenly her own legs gave out—one knee simply buckled, and she rolled over herself onto the grass. Other girls dodged her and jostled for the lead. Her teammates sprinted past, shouting, "Rachel, get up!" She glanced back to where two adults in orange vests were speaking calmly to Darren, their hands on his shoulders to keep him from trying to stand.

7

Two weeks later she was walking from school when Brad idled up along the curb. It had turned cold outside. The days had shortened, and chimney smoke filled the low sky with mesquite. When Brad cranked down his window, a burst of wavy heat escaped the car.

"Get in," he said.

"Are you nuts? Keep driving. Who are you, even?"

"I'll give you a ride. You're really gonna walk up to the Heights in this cold?"

Rachel stopped. She hugged her arms over her chest.

"How do you know where I live?"

A light mist had begun. Brad revved the engine, inching the car forward. On the wheel, his hands were chapped and broken at the knuckles.

"Just get in," he told her. "I'm letting out all the heat."

8

They rode through the park district and into the residential blocks. At a four-way stop, Brad reached over and turned off the stereo. "Your house is up to the left," he said. "But now I have a different idea."

With the gearbox in neutral, he let the car roll slowly backward. Then he shifted into first and turned back toward the lake.

"Stop it," Rachel said. "Brad, turn around. Let me out."

But he kept driving, rolling through stop signs and traffic lights, beyond the school and canal and onto a two-lane highway leading north out of the city. The road wound past lake resorts and thick maple forests. They drove into freezing rain, and the windows fogged up from the inside. Brad took her phone and tucked it in his jacket pocket. The wipers dragged across the windshield and Rachel thought of opening her door and leaping out, but she knew she would only be left worse with no one to help.

Brad turned west onto a county road with no shoulder. "I don't mean to harm you," he said. "I wanted to take you home, I swear it. But I get this yellow light that covers my insides, and the light expands in me and tugs me like I'm bound by ropes. You can't tease me, Rachel. I was going to take you home. Don't tease me anymore, okay? Be a good girl. Don't come around at night and climb my walls or float on my ceiling—I see the way you look at me. Don't cry, Rachel. We're safe. The yellow light is driving now."

On either side of the road were deep, weedy ditches. The highway rose over a bluff, flattened out between fields of chaff. "Brad, slow down."

"Listen here, you little tease." He faced Rachel, his eyes dark and intense. "I'll lift you up with the yellow light. The way I see us, we're already in the air."

He spun the wheel. The tires hissed and Rachel rocked against the passenger door. She closed her eyes and braced her hands against the dash, and the pavement below turned to gravel and the car shimmied, fishtailing along the rocks, and then it steadied. Rachel looked to see they were now riding south. The light of day had sunk behind the hills out her window.

"We're almost there," Brad said.

"Where?"

"We're almost home."

They pulled onto a rutted path enclosed by thick, woolly trees. A small lake or a fishing reservoir came into view, near which sat an old RV camper raised up on blocks. Brad pulled next to it and killed the ignition. He laid on his horn. "This is my Mustang," he told Rachel. "I bought it with money I earned." Then he put the keys in his mouth and left for the camper.

9

Rachel stayed in the car. Rain pattered the roof and dimpled the windshield.

The camper door opened and a man stepped out, but Brad passed him by and went inside. The man wore oil-spotted jeans and two layers of flannel shirts. He was the same man from the hotel pool. He stood there a while looking out into the night, and then he came down for Rachel.

"Let's go inside," he said through the window glass. "Too cold. What's out here for you? Nothing. So come inside. You can call me Jersey. Look—" He pointed down to his bare feet. "Don't make me stand out here forever."

Object

"You're Rachel," said Jersey, drying his hair with a ragged kitchen towel. "What's this about you floating on the ceiling?"

It was warm in the camper. A small space heater hummed between the seats up front. Against one wall was a sagging yellow sofa, and opposite that was a fold-out dining table. There were magazines, empty cans, small bits of machinery smeared in grease. Above the driver's cabin was a lofted bed closed off by one long curtain, thin light glowing around its edges.

"I don't know what that means," Rachel said.

Jersey narrowed his eyes at her. His face was gray and gaunt and cracked like leather. "Brad told me about your pussy," he said. "He described it for me." He breathed through his nose. "I know you're scared, Rachel. You don't have to be scared."

"I don't know where I am."

"You're in my home. They call this the Cloquet Valley," Jersey said, draping the towel over a sink in the kitchenette. "You've probably heard of the Cloquet River, but that's south of here. We're in the uplands. They used to cull this land for timber, but not anymore."

"Brad has my phone. It's in his jacket."

"Right now Brad needs to rest."

"Is he up there, behind that curtain? If he goes to sleep, will you take me home?"

"No," Jersey said. "If you're cold you can have a blanket." He took a seat on the sofa. "Are you hungry, Rachel? You must be hungry. You see that hot plate on the countertop? Yes, that. Now open the cupboard and take down two cans of soup."

Rachel did what he asked.

"There's an iron pot in the cabinet by the floor," Jersey said. "Do you need me to keep giving directions? I'm going to stop talking now and just watch."

11

Rachel made dinner—toast and vegetable soup. She sat at the table while Jersey ate on the sofa. He ate slowly. The night grew calm. A gas generator hummed outside a window of the camper, and rainwater dripped from the surrounding trees. Running away only seemed like an escape into something worse, so Rachel filled the silence by talking.

She told what Brad had done at the region cross-country meet, and Jersey said he knew. It still affected Rachel, and her voice wavered. She said how things might have changed if she'd gone to state as a freshman. All honors aside, she could have been somebody at school, she could have stood out among the crowds, and it would have meant the world to her sisters. Her sisters were from their mother's first marriage, she told Jersey. Their father had died before Rachel was born, and Rachel's own father had left early and she never learned why and sometimes felt like she'd been to blame. Her mother now was distant, medicated, and cheerless. And Rachel wanted to be tough, she said, she wanted to take care of herself, but home to her was like a halfway house and freshman year was like a traffic jam, and even now, in early November, she knew they were in for a long and unforgiving winter.

Jersey had been listening in a stolid, clinical way. Now he reached out between them and snapped his fingers like a battery of firecrackers. "Your life is not remarkable," he said with surprising calm. "You'll find a lot of people with the same problems."

Rachel wiped her nose on the back of her hand.

"Okay," she said.

"I'm going to sleep now. I'm sorry we don't have a guest bed. The floor is clean and there's a blanket." He stood and pulled the chain on an overhead bulb. The cabin went dark but for the glowing coils of the space heater.

The Rift

The next morning Rachel was wearing different clothes—a creamy sweater and knee-length housedress, flesh-colored nylons, and soft leather flats. The clothes were worn thin and smelled of mothballs. They weren't Rachel's clothes. She didn't recall changing into them. Yet she liked how they felt, feathery and warm, and as she stood and looked out the windshield their strangeness passed from her mind like mist through a screen.

Down below, the surface of the lake shone among the white birch and evergreen trees. On the near shore were reeds and scattered boulders, an old boat with its registration numbers faded along the bow. Where were the men? The men were at work. Brad was in the woods by himself, while Jersey had gone off somewhere in the car. Rachel knew this without having to be told.

Before long she got a message that she was meant to clean the inside of the camper. She mixed bleach powder with water from a cloudy jug and scoured grime from every surface, from the driver's cabin up front to a small inoperable bathroom in the rear. She cleaned until her fingertips wrinkled and her nose burned from the bleach solution. The camper had taken on mud, oil, and lint, thistles and animal fur, pebbles, dried leaves, and pine sap—all of which she stuffed into plastic grocery sacks and tied up at the handles. Nothing should remain, she knew.

13

Around dusk she went outside and set the garbage sacks at the front of the camper. All afternoon the men had been working under the hood. At present Jersey had an arm down in the engine, prying something loose with a breaker bar, and Brad was beside him with a penlight.

"It's cold out here," Rachel said, pulling her sleeves down over her hands. "Do you ever go fishing in that lake?"

Brad left them and tried the ignition. The engine roared but then misfired, and the starter made a clicking noise. "Piece of shit," Jersey said. He peered into the engine block, opened a folding knife, and cut something loose. "Timing belt won't catch," he said, holding the penlight to it. "It's all over the pulley. Fucks up everything." He flung it over with the trash.

"What's the timing belt do?" Rachel said.

Jersey let down the prop and settled the hood. He turned the light onto Rachel, then led her away from the camper to a knee-high stump, where she smoothed the dress behind her thighs and sat. "I don't like this uneven color," he said, putting a hand through her hair. "Keep still."

He twisted her hair and pulled it taut, then sawed it off and scattered it in the spotty grass. The blade of his knife was hooked like a scythe, and it reflected orange in the dusky light. A breeze swept over them from the lake. Brad, by then, had come back outside. "I was acting bad yesterday," he said. "I won't do that again."

"What's this for?" Rachel asked.

Jersey stepped back and looked her over. "Hold on," he said. "That looks like shit." He lifted her chin and took off more around her ears. Finally he wiped the blade on his pant leg, brushed the hair from Rachel's neck, and straightened her collar. His hand was very warm. "There," he said. "How's it feel?"

"It's different," she said.

Captain

That second morning Rachel and Jersey went out in the boat. It was a flat-bottom jack boat as plain as a saucer. Before they shoved off, Jersey removed his boots and stripped down to his briefs. "It'll be cold," he said. Without his clothes he was stringy and pale, thin, his ribs like digits. Rachel got down to her sports bra and underwear, and she sat on a thwart up front while Jersey steered with a trolling motor.

The boat rode low in the water. On the floor were perhaps a dozen rocks, some as large as loaves of bread. Jersey explained how this was a glacial lake, connected to other lakes and fed by underground springs. That's how the water stayed so clear. He told Rachel to look over the gunwale, where ten feet down was a school of sterling perch.

At the center of the lake, he cut the motor. "This is when it gets cold," he said, hoisting a rock over his head. "We were never here."

He slammed the rock through the fiberglass floor, and water spewed up like from a burst pipe. Jersey dove into the lake. The water covered Rachel's ankles, so she too dove, and when she looked back only seconds later the boat was a sinking form beneath the surface, and then it was gone.

15

The rest of the day she stayed inside by the space heater. Outside, the sky was gray and cloudless. The men worked in stocking caps and cowhide gloves. By afternoon they had the engine running, and Brad took to removing each wheel with a four-way lug wrench. Together they plugged the tires, but without an air compressor Brad had to fill each one with a small pump like that from a gymnasium. At sundown he called for Rachel to come outside.

He took her around the camper, shining a flashlight over the wheels and engine block, and he reached into a fuse panel and illuminated the side of the cabin with orange running lights. A two-wheeled trailer was hitched to the rear—a tow dolly, Brad explained, for the Mustang.

"I don't care about any of this," Rachel said. "Where's Jersey?"

"My uncle's building a fire down by the water. Aren't you proud of me, Rachel?"

"I just said, I don't care. Take it or leave it, fine with me." She wore a blanket around her shoulders and pulled it tighter. "You have the flashlight. Lead the way."

Jersey was sparking the kindling when they arrived. The logs were stacked like a cabin, and soon the flames curled up and ignited the four sides. A sack of garbage flared up in the center, burning green and pink—scraps of paper, magazines, and food wrappers. Flakes of ash floated up like fireflies in the night.

"Should we sing a song?" Jersey said.

Rachel looked up at him. "That's a really weird thing to say right now."

"I like Bob Seger."

"So weird," Rachel said. "I don't even know who that is."

"You'd recognize his songs."

"'Night Moves,'" said Brad.

Jersey put in another sack of garbage, then another. Rachel saw her jeans and sweater in the flames, her school backpack. What remained shrunk to a hard, dark mass. Small embers tumbled down into the coals. She rubbed her eyes, which stung from the smoke.

16

Rachel's third morning would be their last in the woods. She first remembered sitting on the stump outside while Brad fastened twine around her neck in the style of a halter. It was very cold, and her breath made clouds in the early light.

He led her into the trees, where together they collected rabbit traps from among the root systems and tall grass. The traps—rough metal, more than a dozen in total—were spring loaded, and those that weren't closed already Brad set off by stabbing a twig between their teeth. He navigated by instinct, though Rachel stumbled over roots and snagged the tether on low-hanging branches. When she strayed, the twine would tighten and she would gasp for air.

Only one trap contained a rabbit, its ankle snapped and the white of its bone exposed. Brad and Rachel carried the traps by their chains until they dropped them in a pile outside the camper. "Me and you'll clean these," he said, untying the halter. "I'll skin the rabbit, you don't have to do that. And then say goodbye to all this."

"Goodbye to all this," said Rachel.

Light Me Up

Soon after that, she escaped. Her escape was quick. It had to be.

Back in the camper she had a vision of herself in the car, driving alone on the two-lane highway into Duluth. The scene was vivid in her mind—sunlight glinting between the trees off the icy waters of Lake Superior—and to reach that point she played the events backward as she imagined them: the car, the keys, a fight, seduction. Now she stood in the kitchenette, fixing the men their coffee.

When she brought it to them at the dining table, she laced fingers with Jersey. It was an odd gesture, her first time doing so. Although he shook her hand away, across the table the blood rose in Brad's cheeks. Rachel knew there was the question of who would possess her first. She moved closer and pressed a hip into Jersey's shoulder.

"What is this?" said Brad. "You told me she was mine."

"Get away," Jersey said, shoving her aside. "Keep to yourself."

"Did he tell you that? It's not true," Rachel said. "Jersey, show him. Touch me like last night." She lifted the blouse over her shoulders. "I want Brad to watch."

"She's lying," Jersey said, just as Brad yanked away his chair and dropped him to the floor. Their boots scrabbled over the carpet. Brad took the top and pummeled Jersey in the ribs—they grappled and turned one another, hitting the table and spilling coffee across the wall. Jersey shucked him and got to his knees, but Brad pounced again and landed an elbow in Jersey's kidney.

"Stop!" Rachel shouted.

Brad looked up. She swung the hot plate into the side of his face. He rolled down to the carpet, unmoving.

"You little cunt," Jersey said.

"He was hurting you," Rachel said. "Stay back, please."

She shoved the hot plate, but Jersey deflected it with an open hand. "Rachel, you fucked up," he said, unclipping the folding knife from his belt. "Get on the floor." She pried the lid off the bleach canister and scattered it forward. When he lunged out, she batted his wrist and the knife went loose. Jersey fell to his knees, coughing and brushing at his eyes. And in that moment Rachel fished the keys from Brad's pocket and ran outside to the Mustang.

The car was a manual transmission. Rachel mashed the pedals and hammered the gears, and though she started it once, it soon shuddered and died. She tried the ignition again, dropped the clutch and slammed the gas, and the car jolted forward into the side of the camper.

She got out. The hood of the car was folded back and its windshield had bloomed into a spiderweb pattern. Jersey was throwing his shoulder into the camper door, now pinned shut. He put his elbow through the window glass, though the door didn't budge. And although Rachel's vision was blurry and her knees were weak, she knew to run up the rutted trail to a county road, and from there to keep running, until miles later she stopped at a crossroad and flagged the first truck to pass.

Transitions

That winter Rachel moved in with her oldest sister down in St. Paul. The sister, Bethany, was twenty-eight and recently divorced. Her married name had been Briggs, and a social worker suggested Rachel adopt Briggs as well. Although her name never appeared in the papers, Brad and Jersey's arrest had become an ongoing narrative in the statewide media. Briggs was meant to protect Rachel's anonymity, should it ever come to that.

For several months Bethany took Rachel with her to separation support groups held in community halls and church basements. These rooms were dimly lit and smelled of mildew, with dry cookies and too-strong coffee. And the women were sad, victimized, shattered in ways that resisted healing. To them, redemption seemed foggy and beyond reach. Soon Bethany recognized the error of exposing Rachel to such a culture.

"We should go to a basketball game instead," she said one night as they were putting on their coats to leave the apartment. "Probably I've gotten all I can from those meetings."

"I have homework," Rachel said. "Can we afford tickets, anyway?"

"We'll scalp them cheap. Bring your homework. You realize you're my best friend," Bethany said. "I don't want to sit around inside my own head either."

19

That May the state track meet was held on one of the college campuses there in the city. Rachel had qualified for the 3,200-meter run, and as it happened she was placed in a heat with one of the seniors from her old school. The senior looked at her oddly at first, as if Rachel's was a face familiar yet altogether changed. "Rachel?" said the senior. "Your hair's so short. Where have you been?" But then they were made to take their lanes, and the race began.

Rachel stayed up front until the seventh lap, when she began her sprint and was taken by a vast yellow heat. The heat pressed in from the sides of her vision, blurring the stands, the lane markers, and the infield grass. She felt herself swept upward, lifted over the track. The fact of inertia brought her to a halt. Ahead, the scoreboard timer had stopped. A nearby pole vaulter had frozen with his pole in a perfect arc.

A familiar voice appeared to her in a sermon, though it wasn't made of words, but light. The light suspended Rachel in place. It burned away everything and she felt its warmth, though she herself did not burn. The light was energy, it was electric. It was a tactile force. The light was sunrise, sunset, the gradient of leaves as the branches are stripped bare. And then the light dimmed out and Rachel came back down. Her momentum took her into a middle lane, where she caught a spike on the track and tumbled to the ground.

The other runners passed her by. She stood and hobbled to the inside lane. Her shin was scraped, blood collecting in her sock, but she finished the race. Afterward, she allowed two lane-timers to carry her by the shoulders to a first-aid booth. Her old teammate, she was told, had lost steam in the final hundred meters and drawn up fourth.

Did You See Me?

Something maneuvered Rachel. She felt warmth in dark corners and would go to them. She heard bells in the distance that no one else heard. She would take down flags in strangers' yards or turn books upside down in the school library, and when questioned why she couldn't explain. She moved in odd directions as though pulled by a polar magnet.

"I want you to try taking medicine," said her counselor, a prim man in wide paisley ties who'd been appointed by the state.

"I don't want medicine," Rachel said. "I'm afraid I'll gag."

"It will help you," said her counselor.

"I need to ask someone first."

"Who is this 'someone' you refer to?"

21

In the summers Bethany taught at a language camp held further south along the river. Rachel joined her as an aide, working one summer in the kitchen and the next hosting conversation circles in French. The days were long—all sunlight, warm air, lush foliage. Boys flirted with Rachel and she flirted back, but when they were alone she became flustered and panicky. One night at campfire, a boy named Jason Kurtz came up from behind and caressed the back of Rachel's neck, and she turned and shoved him over a wooden bench.

"It frightened me," she told Bethany later. "Like inside I got all cold, but outside I was burning up. I was sweating, like all of a sudden. I don't even like Jason Kurtz. What right does he have to touch me?"

"He likes you. You don't have to like him back," Bethany said. "But believe me, what he did was innocent."

"You don't have to tell me that," Rachel said. "Jason and I are friends—he's shy and sincere. But I'd sooner step into a tornado than let him or anyone …" She was shaking just talking about it. "I understand it, okay, but I don't want it."

22

Rachel Briggs continued running. She grew another four inches by her junior year, and her strides lengthened and she improved her posture. Running wasn't a metaphor. It didn't mean avoidance or escape. Running was just something that called Rachel to the present moment. It changed her chemically, like it untied a knot around her chest and drained the tension through her fingertips and toes, until inside she was pleasantly empty. She won races too, but the winning never mattered so much as the emptying.

23

Jersey died in prison the spring of Rachel's junior year. He'd been of the lowest class of inmates, those whose offenses involved minors. One night he was stabbed and had bled out before the prison guards found him in the morning. As for his assailant, it wasn't known. It didn't matter. The news came through Bethany, who'd learned in a phone call from their mother. "That means the end of his appeal," Bethany said. "It means the end for everything with that man."

"His name was Jersey," Rachel said. She'd returned to their apartment after track practice. It was unseasonably warm, and she wore thin polyester shorts and a school t-shirt showing athletic feet with wings.

"You can cry," said Bethany. "Even if you're confused. It's all right."

"I don't need to," Rachel said, filling a glass with filtered water from the fridge. She asked what would become of the other man, the nephew, but Bethany didn't know. And in truth, Rachel had nearly forgotten Brad Van Laecken, which was close enough, she felt, to forgiving him.

Tried and True

And Rachel fit in at school—she blended in. She made friends, and she dressed nice, and some weekends she and her girlfriends would go to games or the mall or to outdoor markets in the city center. In the summer before her senior year, she saw Darren Hunt at the state fair, in the grandstand at an evening concert. At a break between songs, Darren joined her at a railing along the bleachers. "How are you?" he said.

"Do I know you?" Rachel said. But of course she knew him. Darren had hardly changed. He was still pale and gangly, awkwardly attentive. "Listen, I can't talk right now," she said. "Those are my friends. It's nothing personal. Don't tell anyone you saw me, okay? I'm someone different now."

"But where did you go?" he asked.

Rachel told Darren it was nice seeing him and that she remembered him fondly, then she slipped away before the band returned for its encore. She took the bus home early, before her curfew. Back at the apartment, she changed into her shorts and running shoes, and despite

Bethany's worries she took to the lighted trails around the city's chain of lakes, as she often did, lithe as a doe, watchful like an owl.

25

Fall of Rachel's senior year her mother parked in the garage and ran her engine overnight. A neighbor found her two days later. Rachel hadn't been home in three years—time enough that she no longer thought of it as home. But she and Bethany drove up without any ado, and the night before the funeral they and their two other sisters walked around the canal by Lake Superior and went out for pizza. Their server was a blonde girl Rachel's own age, and when she came for their drink order, she halted and put a finger to her chin.

"Rachel? Is that you? It's me, Helen," she said. "Rachel, it's been ages. What school are you at now? Are these your sisters?" Everyone made their introductions. Helen Voight had grown into a woman, cheery and self-assured. "I sure miss you, Rachel," she said. "I feel like I haven't seen you since … it was the Fourth of July … there was that older boy. Do you remember?"

"I do remember," Rachel said.

"Who's this older boy, Rachel?" said one of her sisters. "See, Helen, Rachel doesn't tell us about her boyfriends."

"Helen, did you know I used to be a restaurant server?" Bethany said abruptly. "You don't know the place. It was a sandwich shop down the road, but it's gone now."

Then the sisters got to talking about places in town that no longer existed, the empty buildings and unfamiliar storefronts, and Helen left to put in their orders. Rachel smiled and nodded and kept good company, and later she and Helen hugged and promised to find one another online, although Rachel knew they'd forget that promise before the night even ended.

Even If You Don't

That Christmas Bethany's boyfriend invited her and Rachel to spend the holiday with his family. They gathered at a wide, three-story house in one of the affluent suburbs. The family's foyer was open and airy, a Christmas tree rising up beside the staircase with glistening ornaments and strings of garland. Dinner was goose, parsley, and potatoes, a dozen other things. The boyfriend's father played piano while the mother sang carols, something Rachel would have only imagined in a holiday movie.

They were in the den when Bethany's boyfriend produced a gift from his jacket pocket. He tossed it across the room to Rachel. "From all of us," he said. "Open it."

Rachel undid the bow. She peeled back the paper and held out a small jeweler's box, which she opened to find a bright gold necklace with an anchor pendant.

"Oh, come on, don't cry," Bethany said. "It's just a little gift. Say thank you."

"I wasn't going to cry," Rachel said. And she laughed to show how far from tears she actually was. "You were teasing, I know. Thank you." She held up the necklace for everyone to see. Holiday bulbs reflected off the tines of the anchor. Put it on, the family urged her, but she pretended not to hear. "It really is pretty," she said. "I'll carry it with me, okay?"

(SEA CHANGES AND COELACANTHS)

Before there was life, there was water. You read this in a textbook and for years the world lost its mystery. Your life came to seem engineered, subject only to the whims of utility. Then you heard in the news of a recent discovery: a school of fish perfectly preserved in the side of a mountain. Prehistoric fish, with blades for gills and thorns for teeth. And everything was mysterious again. Weekends you set out for the canyon, hiking on trails long ago trampled to dust. You would think how water once covered this land. Proof was in the sediment of the sandstone walls. No longer troubled by the heat, you saw yourself as the vulture does: high noon under the sun, leaving no shadow, softening flesh to be torn from the bone. And you wondered—if the water should rise again, say, at this very instant? Well, you would die swiftly and without ceremony. Or maybe you would survive. You might surface on a great lake, your life preserver an uprooted barrel cactus. At low tide you would wade to shore, stop your wounds with sap, forage on beetles and berries. You might mark the days on the trunk of an ironwood, carve messages into the sand. Moss would grow thick along a freshwater stream. And you would craft a spear from a fallen branch. Stalk the shallows watching for the glint of scales.

FRICASSEE

In the four months he'd been out of work, Chip Duggins had formed a theory of marriage. Marriage, he decided, was like scramble format golf—best ball—in which you and your partner void one another's flaws and pardon each other from the rough. For example, say you launch your drive into the lake, but your partner lands hers in the middle of the fairway. Bang, no penalty. Or your partner slices her approach into the trees, but yours drops just short of the pin. Again, sitting pretty. Marriage was like that. If you're both shooting straight, super, and if not, at least the other has time to iron out any kinks of technique.

This theory served Chip well when unemployment was still new like summer vacation. But given time he came to see a flaw in his logic, namely that you and your partner were only ever as good as the one aiming for par. A better analogy might be that marriage is a doubles tennis match, in which only together can you cover the entire court. Or it's a tandem bicycle on a mountain path, where you risk a horrific crash if one stops pedaling too long to gawk at the trees.

Ask Kaitlyn, Chip's wife, and marriage wasn't *like* anything. It was a partnership, plain and simple. And the only truth to be derived from Chip's theories was that he'd been sitting around too long thinking, not working, in turn failing to hold up his end of the partnership.

On the morning of their fifth anniversary, Chip made a plan to restore Kaitlyn's confidence. While she was applying mascara in the bathroom mirror, he slid in behind her and said that tonight he would surprise her by cooking a special dinner: chicken fricassee.

She said that since he'd just told her, he'd ruined the surprise. "And it's pronounced frick-uh-see," she added.

"Oh?" said Chip, sitting on the rim of the tub with his recipe card. "I thought it was *assy*. Frick-assy."

"Fricassee," Kaitlyn said. "Do you even know what that is?"

"Nope, but it sounds fancy. Case in point, I didn't know how to say it."

Kaitlyn capped her mascara. Her phone was near the sink, and she checked the time. Kaitlyn worked at the airport, as a server in the Skymasters Club. She was lean and purposeful, with fine posture and taut skin. Chip, by contrast, was athletic but shapeless, with more than one food stain on his bathrobe. Most recently he'd been a hotel night manager, but at age thirty he'd pretty well burned out working hospitality. Since then he was thinking about substitute teaching, but he only wanted to teach gym class, and now it was summer, anyway.

"Maybe we should do fricassee together, another time," Kaitlyn said. "It's a weeknight. I might need to stay late."

"Not tonight, Katie. Most people only get one five-year anniversary."

She turned up her hands, like, *What am I supposed to do?*

"Let me try this, please," Chip said. "I've been off lately, but tonight I'll get things right. My gift to you: fricassee, potatoes, some other crap, red wine."

"White wine, if it's chicken."

"Just you wait, I'll figure this out. You'll be surprised."

"If you really want to surprise me," said Kaitlyn, "you can look for a job."

"Touché," Chip said, going to the sink and giving her a full squeeze from behind. "Dinner at six, trust me. When have I ever let you down, yet, today?"

§

That morning at the grocery store Chip zigzagged among the aisles, working his way down the recipe card. The basic ingredients they had at home already, and for the others he chose the freshest he could find—cooking oil imported from Florence, free-range chicken pieces, organic vegetables. Gourmet everything!

Then he came upon the last ingredient: *fresh ground basil.*

"Spices and seasonings," said a woman stocking the greens cooler.

"Tried it," Chip said. "I tried the canisters by the nuts and tea leaves too."

"And there was no basil?"

"Not the kind I need," said Chip, handing over the recipe card.

The woman had silver hair and red-rimmed eyes. She took a pair of glasses from her store apron and studied the card. Chip explained there was nothing labeled *fresh* in the spice aisle, nor *ground*, for that matter. He was being too literal, the woman said. "It's all basil, one and the same. And one-quarter teaspoon is all. For that amount you might as well use grass clippings."

"I don't think so," Chip said. "I'm doing this by the book."

The woman dropped her chin and examined him over the frame of her glasses. The automatic sprayers switched on, hissing a fine mist over the greens. "Sure, be a perfectionist," she said, returning the card. "Go to a co-op if you care so much. Do you need cabbage? I have this entire pallet of cabbage. No? Then goodbye."

From there Chip drove to a package shop, where he bought two bottles of the second-least-expensive wine. Back in the car he searched "co-op" on his phone, but it was a broad term. He fussed with the map feature until he gave up and tore into a box of fruit snacks. Overhead, the sun was big and surly. Further down the parking lot was a new store, a golfing boutique called Duffer's Dream. Its windows featured a grease painting of a golf cart half-buried in sand, along with the message SINK PUTTS, NOT BUTTS. He walked over and went inside.

The air in Duffer's Dream was cool and tranquil. At first Chip combed through the patterned shorts and polos, attempting the motions of a serious customer. In time he worked his way to the clearance items in back, where he picked out a Big Bertha Diablo, an oversized driver with a clubface the size of a skillet.

"Excellent choice," said a young salesman out of nowhere. He was tan with spiky blond hair, a stiff collar, and tiny gold studs in each ear. "The Diablo: major wood, heh."

"I can't buy anything," Chip said. "My wife would have my balls if I dropped …" He checked the price tag. "Three hundred bucks on a golf club."

"I could give it to you for two ninety," said the boy, Percy according to his nametag.

"No thanks," Chip said.

"Two eighty-five."

"No."

"Sure, Diablo is top of the line," Percy said. "But here's a question: Would you bike the Tour de France in training wheels? Nah, man, you'd be crazy. Would you play a game of five-on-five in flip-flops? No, never, come on. What's the lesson? You can't put a price on quality, dude."

"Can't do it," Chip said, returning the club to its display. "My wife. It's our anniversary."

This new information threw Percy off his spiel. He paused with his mouth open and a hand in the air. "Anniversary … of marriage? We should celebrate," he said. "Do you like partying? I like partying. Tell you what, how about me and you, let's grip it and rip it."

Before Chip could say no or ask what, Percy grabbed the Diablo and yelled to another salesman that they'd be out back. He led Chip through a small stock room and kicked open a fire-exit door, though no alarm sounded. Outside was a patch of fake, feathery sod. A few dozen balls littered the ground. Drooping nets formed a cage, separating them from where the concrete sloped down to a freeway embankment.

"Check it, dude!" said Percy. "This is our demo range. I built it myself! That's not true." He gathered up the balls and placed one on a rubberized tee. "Happy anniversary," he said, handing Chip the Diablo. "You're up, champ."

"Wow," Chip said. "Just wow. Thanks, Percy."

"My friends call me P-Dawg," he said, settling into a canvas sling chair.

Chip approached the tee. He took a deep breath and set his stance, kneading the grip of the club. Down on the freeway, cars hummed like a stream over pebbles. Chip hauled off and drilled his tee shot, heaving the net forward. The club rang pitch perfect.

At Percy's urging, he set up another shot, then another. The club was swift, and Chip handled it deftly. He got to talking. "I can't miss. This thing's got a face like a hockey stick. Hoo-ee! What is this, aluminum, titanium? Sure is light." Finally his shoulders began feeling heavy. "That was boss," he said. "I haven't swung in a while. I'm forming a blister already."

"Seriously, a blister? We get inside, we'll find you a nice glove."

Chip passed the club to Percy. "You got a handicap?"

"Don't laugh," said Percy, teeing up and taking a practice swing. "Plus twenty-eight. You?"

"I drink too much and my game goes to shit by the sixth hole."

Percy snorted a laugh and shanked his drive. "Well played." And then he took his own turn at the tee box, pounding his drives into the net. "Boom, moonshot!" he yelled. "Pow! That one woulda smashed the glass at JOANN Fabrics. Fore!" His voice cracked with the color commentary. The sun moved over the store, leaving the two of them in shade.

"Hey, P-Dawg," Chip said. "You guys aren't hiring, are you?"

Percy gave him a painted-on grin. "You can list me as a reference," he said, offering a fist for bumping. "So where's the better half? How come you're here alone on your anniversary?"

"Wife's working today. I'm on dinner duty." Chip explained about Kaitlyn and the fricassee. The trouble, he said, was that he hardly knew what fricassee was, and he wouldn't truly know until he started the recipe. Add to that, the fresh ground basil problem. He said he was going to try a co-op next, once he figured out what and where a co-op was.

Percy ran a finger around his ear canal. "I know a co-op, across town by my mom's house. You can give me a ride, I'll show you. Not that I live with my mom. I do, but it's temporary," he said. "So, now, let's go inside and look at the gloves. You don't *have* to buy one, but I am paid on commission."

§

On the freeway Percy began futzing with the radio. He tuned to a hip-hop station and attempted falsetto harmony. Chip hit the preset button for classic rock. Percy scanned ahead to conservative talk, then country ballads, then he turned off the stereo completely.

"Pee-ew!" he said, pinching his nose. "Smells like dead animal in here."

"No, it doesn't. Just some groceries in the backseat." Chip cranked down his window. "I think you're sitting on my fruit snacks."

"On purpose. Soften 'em up."

They crossed a long bridge, six lanes wide. When a semi-trailer moved past, the recipe card floated off the dashboard and whizzed toward the driver-side window. Percy grabbed, missed, and punched Chip in the ear. A speedy red car squeaked its horn. "Got it," Percy said, digging the card from a grocery sack. "Close call."

Another gust came through and pasted the job application over Percy's face. Chip tried snatching it and got a finger in Percy's nose. The application fluttered out the open window, danced along the pavement behind them, and disappeared beneath a white SUV.

"You don't want to work at Duffer's Dream anyway," Percy said, peeling open a package of fruit snacks. "Minimum wage and you gotta hustle for commission. Besides, you're a grown man. I'm just a bro living with his mom trying to get back into community college. Exit here."

Percy's co-op was a low, grimy building with a dirt parking lot. Its rain gutters sagged under the weight of moss, and inside was the odor of things fermenting or slowly decaying. The overhead lights were off to conserve energy, and a circular fan rotated near the produce cooler. Beside the checkout counter, a tabby cat rested on a bale of straw.

"Where are we, P-Dawg?" said Chip.

"Barn? You're on your own," Percy said. "Nachos, nachos, where are the nachos?"

Of the packaged goods, Chip recognized none of the brands—they were all *Garden* this, *Nature* that, *Whole* and *Green* and *Pure*. The spices, once he located them, were sorted by glass jars with the names stenciled onto plain white labels. When a girl in a loose-fitting tunic and a co-op lanyard approached, Chip explained the problem: anniversary dinner, chicken fricassee, fresh ground basil.

"Basil," said the girl, plucking a jar from the shelf. "So what's the stress?"

Chip showed her the recipe card. "I need it *fresh*," he said, "and *ground*."

"Let's see that," said the girl, sweeping a string of hair from her eyes. Her face and neck were brushed with freckles, and she had long, delicate fingers. "Oh, wait," she said. "You're thinking is *ground basil* different from regular basil, the way *groundhog* is different from hog."

"Maybe," Chip said. "Is it?"

"No."

"No what, the basil or the groundhog?"

"Well, hello," said Percy, now cradling the cat in his arms.

"You found Jenkins," said the girl. "Jenkins is the cat." She reached out with both hands and massaged its ears. "My name's Clover."

"Chip's making dinner for his wife," Percy said. "I'm helping. We're looking for something called basil. I'm Percy, by the way. You can call me P-Dawg."

"No, I'll call you Percy," said Clover. "Just get that basil. It's all the same." She took the cat and set it on the floor. "Go on now. You're dismissed. You'll do fine with the fricassee. Most people could cook that blindfolded. So what now, why are you making that face?"

"I'm scared," Chip said, rolling the spice jar between his palms. "This is getting complicated. I just eat cereal. That card says I need a meat thermometer? Kaitlyn, my wife, she's going to think I'm beyond hope. I haven't worked since March. I'm spinning my wheels here. Fricassee, fresh ground basil? I haven't even showered today."

Clover was fidgeting with her fabric bracelets. She blinked a few times in succession. "Wow, you *are* screwed," she said. "Okay, I know someone who can help. Her name's Clover, she works at a bistro too, and she's a mean scratch cook." She looked between Chip and Percy, waiting for a response. "*Me*, you dummies. I'm Clover. I'll help. Jenkins comes too. We're a package deal."

§

Chip regained the freeway, Clover riding shotgun and Percy in back with the cat. Cars were swarming for the late-afternoon rush, and road construction made matters worse. In time traffic came to a standstill. "This little dude is tame," said Percy. "Who's a sleepy kitty?"

"He got into the chamomile ointment," Clover said. "Oof, kinda stinks in here, like something died. Chip, you have pans and utensils, right?"

"Right."

"Because no offense, but you didn't know what basil was."

"Basil is a culinary herb," said Percy, "often used in Italian coo … coo-is … cuisine." He scrolled down on his phone. "Also called Saint Joseph's Wort. You don't get warts from eating it, do you?"

"You two need a lesson on where your food comes from," said Clover. "Look at all these fruit snack wrappers. Do you have any idea what you're putting in your bodies? Chip, you're eating too many carbs, Percy too much salt and fake sugar. I can tell just by looking."

"This wine is like boiling back here," Percy announced.

Chip exited onto a frontage road, and from there he steered through byways and backstreets leading them home. He parked in the driveway, and they all went inside and spread the groceries over the kitchen counter.

"Uh-oh," said Chip.

"Uh-oh what?" said Percy.

"Uh-oh this." He hung the package of chicken between his thumb and forefinger. The meat had turned gamy in the midday sun, its flesh cloudy and gray. And the mushrooms had darkened, the green peppers gone loose. The entire array smelled of carcass. Jenkins appeared on the counter nosing around a plastic sack.

"Well, we tried," Percy said. "Now what? Chip, can you write a sonnet?"

Clover assessed the food. "Unsalvageable," she said, wagging her head. "Chicken, you died in vain. I'm sorry, Chip, but there will be no fricassee tonight. Seriously, though? Fricassee is salty, sloppy, and it'll clog your veins with sludge. We can still impress your wife. Is that her?" She indicated a small portrait on the refrigerator door.

"*That?*" Chip said. "No, that's Franken Berry. I'm saving box tops for a t-shirt. *That's* Kaitlyn." He pointed to a different picture, in which Kaitlyn was outdoors in a backless dress. "That's from a friend's wedding last fall."

"Nuh-uh," Percy cried. "That's Kaitlyn?"

"She's gorgeous!" Clover said. "And you're kind of ... well, you're in a down phase right now. Dinner tonight is how we raise you up. We can't quit now. Let's focus."

She sent Percy to dump the spoiled food out beside the house. Meanwhile, she and Chip ransacked the cupboards. They collected all the staples—greens, grains, and nonperishables—while Clover pitched taffy and cookie wafers and bright orange crackers into the trash. Chip sorted through a pantry only to find two jars of basil, which he subtly tucked behind the other spices. Once Percy returned, they'd laid their findings on the counter: pasta and rice, instant potatoes, seasoning packets, canned goods of indeterminate vintage.

"Okay, this can work," Clover said. "We need this, this, not this ..." She said they could make pasta bowls—a mishmash, twice-baked with a potato base. "Chip, we need a can opener, a wooden spoon, and a strainer. Percy, you just, uh, here—" She handed him a sleeve of bagels. "Pluck out all these raisins. And wash your hands!"

They got to work. Clover set the stovetop dials and salted a large pot of water. At her request, Chip drained cans of loose corn and butter beans, then squashed two wrinkly old tomatoes with a meat tenderizer. Once the water came to a boil, he measured two cups for the instant potatoes. Clover grasped a handful of spaghetti and gauged its thickness.

"Time out. I'm wrecking these bagels," Percy said, wandering off down a hallway.

"I think he likes you," Chip said.

"And I like him," Clover said. "Restrained, with duct tape over his mouth, tossed in the back of a towncar. Actually, he's not that bad. He's trying his best. Like you."

She directed Chip to wash out two stoneware bowls, into which she spread the creamy potatoes. It looked weird, but she insisted it was part of the plan. She then misted the potatoes with butter from a spray bottle, set them to bake, and placed the tomato-and-vegetable mixture over low heat.

Percy bounded back into the kitchen with a pair of tweezers. "I'm gonna use these suckers on the bagels," he said. "Why am I doing this, Clover?"

"So you'll stay out of my way."

Percy shrugged and kept at it. "Does kitty want raisins?" he said, and Clover slapped his hand with a plastic spatula.

They began the pasta. In addition to spaghetti, they had little colored bowties, which darted and spun in the bubbles of the big iron pot. It got steamy in the kitchen. Chip switched on an exhaust fan, which buzzed and crackled, then rained down sparks onto the stovetop. But it was fine. He scooped black debris from the pot using the strainer like a tiny pool skimmer.

Soon the potatoes had baked to a peanut-like brown. But they weren't done yet, said Clover. She had Chip drain the pasta, stir it with the vegetable sauce, and dump it over the potatoes, which now served as a base. Percy was at the ready with a zip-top bag of shredded cheese. Now the bowls go back in the oven, Clover said, reaching out with a potholder.

"Wait," said Chip. "If I may." He produced a white leather glove from his back pocket, snipped off the price tag, and nodded to Percy. Wearing it like a mitt, he returned the two bowls to the oven. "That actually burned my fingertips. That wasn't a smart thing to do," he said. "Okay, now I have an idea: bread pudding. Those bagel pieces, the raisins, old banana, that half-and-half. And, Clover, permission to take those wafers from the garbage?"

Chip's idea was to mash everything together. He used the meat tenderizer, then a whisk. When he sampled the pudding, his face puckered, stretched, and wilted. Clover nudged past him and splashed something dark into the pudding. "Vanilla," she explained. "In case you wanna taste your food."

§

They were setting the table when Kaitlyn's truck sounded up the driveway. "Look sharp, you two," Chip said. "Here she comes." The side door opened and Kaitlyn's keys plunked down on an entryway table. She turned into the kitchen, gave a start, and halted in place.

"Katie, hear me out," Chip began. "I wanted nothing more than to please you tonight. You deserve the best—that's why I came up with the fricassee idea. But there is no fricassee. Please don't take this as a measure of my devotion. We have something even better."

Kaitlyn's ponytail had fallen loose, and her shirt was untucked. Her shoulders slumped, and she appeared tired. At her feet, the cat flopped onto its side, batting an untied shoelace. Then an egg timer rang, and Clover and Percy took the pasta bowls from the oven. When Kaitlyn saw the dinner, she turned without a word, grabbed her keys, and left out the side door.

"I know," Chip said. "I should follow her."

And he did follow her. He went out into the driveway, where she stood leaning against the hood of her truck. He said her name, but she raised a hand and shushed him.

"You said your piece. Now it's my turn." This was rock bottom, Kaitlyn told him. Nothing was what she might have hoped for five years ago. Chip wasn't being serious, he wasn't being resilient, and he'd put an onus on her. "Do you think I *want* to be a waitress?" she said.

When could she quit her job and find something new? Not now, not while Chip had no income. She told him all the things he already knew. She wasn't giving up, she said, if that's what he was worried about. But sometimes she felt like tugging her hair or clawing her eyes in frustration.

She opened the truck door and climbed in. Chip backed away to let her go. But she emerged toting a plastic sack from the Skymasters Club, the sides of which stretched with two Styrofoam containers.

"What's that?"

"What do you think?" She dropped the tailgate and opened a container. It held a glop of mushrooms, celery and peppers, chicken meat and gray gravy. The stuff was warm, sweating up the inside of the Styrofoam lid.

"That's what fricassee looks like? Uck."

"Surprise," Kaitlyn said. "Don't mistake this as forgiveness. I doubted you, and it shouldn't be that way. Don't force me to make back-up plans." She stopped him before he could apologize. "No more words," she said. "Actions. Like today, but better."

They ate. The first bites were really good, but then the fricassee got messy. Gravy slopped around and spilled on the tailgate. Their plastic silverware bent and snapped. Chip remarked that fricassee, in fact, tasted like shit, and Kaitlyn said she could have told him that this morning. They both quit before they were full.

"Who are those kids in the kitchen? Actually, hold that thought." Kaitlyn wiped her lips on her shirtsleeve. "You know what I could stand? Chocolate milkshake from the Scoop Shack."

"Yes," Chip said. "You drive. My car has a smell."

"You're forgetting something." Kaitlyn nodded to the front bay window, where indiscreetly Percy and Clover were peeking around the curtains.

"Young love," Chip said. "Let them be. They won't go hungry."

IN MY LIFE WITH CARL LEHMANN

Trevor Thomas was like me! He was a knobby, lanky fellow forever clad in flannel shirts and black jeans. We were classmates at the Art Institute, and he lived behind me in the Mission District. With his mile-a-minute strides, he could reach my front door in seconds. "Howdy, Carl," he'd say, blowing through like a gale. "Later, Carl!" Where'd you go, Trevor Thomas?

And what an artist! His trade and truest passion was lithography. "Zinc and ink," he was fond of saying. "Rock that roller and put it to bed, what a relief," which were printmaking jokes. He often smelled of lacquer and solvents, but everyone smelled in those days. At least Trevor Thomas had the lithographs to show for it.

We were in our twenties then, and life was like the slow ascent of a rollercoaster. Sit tight, huge thrills ahead. You wanted someone like Trevor Thomas beside you. His joy was infectious, and he could make anyone into a believer. For example, his Minty Coke idea.

One afternoon he burst into my living room with a small foam cooler and a brown sack. "You're in for a treat, old boy," he said, stuffing a manila folder in my hands. "Meet me in the kitchen, ten minutes." The folder was marked as a business proposal, though it contained only drawings. Spearmint, water mint, peppermint, catnip—lovingly rendered but lacking all context. When enough time passed, I set the folder aside and joined Trevor Thomas in the kitchen.

Hello! It was like I'd entered a TV game show: the curtains were drawn, candles flickered, and on the table were four ceramic mugs, each with a small card featuring a question mark made from glitter and white glue. And Trevor Thomas? He wore a velvet hat, dark vest, and white gloves, and he was twirling a stout black wand. "What," I said, "is this?"

"It's a taste test, you kook. That's what the coffee mugs are for."

"Where'd you get those duds?"

"Thrift store," he said. "I think a magician passed away."

He gave me the rules. I was to sample the mugs, each of which contained a dark soda, then answer one final question. Easy enough. He rapped the table with his wand and urged me to begin.

The soda in the first mug was fizzy and sweet. It tasted like Coca-Cola, and I said as much to Trevor Thomas. "It is Coca-Cola," he said. "But that's not how the game works. Drink up, man."

The second mug was Tab. You could tell because it had the vintage of a two-liter bottle left in the sun for a week. The third was root beer, my favorite, but for the sake of the game I said nothing about it.

"Let's pause," said Trevor Thomas. "Good pops, right? Of course they are. But they could be better—fresher, more tang. Something's missing, but what? One mug to go, my friend. Don't keep me waiting."

The final mug had an oily sheen, like medicine. I swirled it like a wine glass, but that only muddied the soda. Meanwhile, Trevor Thomas was shifting his weight and creaking the floorboards. He nodded for me to trust him, so I tilted the mug and downed it in one gulp. The soda was mentholated. It was so spicy it seemed hot. My eyes watered and my throat burned, and something globular stuck in my gullet. "It's good," I croaked. "That was ... special."

"Now," said Trevor Thomas, "which one contains a tablespoon of Vicks VapoRub?"

"Probably the last one," I said, wiping my nose on my sleeve.

One by one, he turned over the glitter cards. Written on the fourth one, it said, MINTY COKE. "Correct," said Trevor Thomas. "Carl, you're the first fan of Minty Coke! You won the taste test. We all won!" He flipped his magician's hat onto my head, took my hands, and led me in a jig. "Let's make a toast—champagne all around. You don't have champagne, do you?"

"No," I said. My cupboards were constantly empty in those days. I didn't have rice or soup, let alone champagne. "Make some Minty Coke."

And that's what he did, mixing it up like a float. I poured more root beer and we toasted one another. "Yowza," he said, wincing. "Prototype. Maybe an acquired taste." But he mixed up another batch and drank it just the same. Once we'd finished the sodas and opened up the curtains, he held his vial of craft-store glitter to the light. "You know, you could probably put glitter in Minty Coke," he said. "Shoot, now I gotta rewrite that whole proposal."

"That's the burden of genius," I said.

But the lithographs—there was genius! The one I remember best was of Willie Mays in his batting stance, a reproduction from an old baseball card. Trevor Thomas used that image for Bring Mays Back, his campaign to spur Willie Mays from retirement. The project was massive—stickers, buttons, even t-shirts. Best of all, Trevor Thomas xeroxed the image and affixed fliers to every tree and light post within the panhandle of Golden Gate Park.

Eventually the fliers went missing, faded in the rain, or were defaced with mustaches and googly eyes. It seemed no one gave much thought to Bring Mays Back. One problem was that the card dated to Willie Mays's rookie year, when the Giants were still in New York. The NY on his cap might have confused people. But also, this was the 1980s and Willie Mays was over fifty years old, long retired.

Later on we went to a house party where one of the family room walls was pasted over with Bring Mays Back fliers. The dude hosting the party thought himself an art collector and said he adhered to the Dada and Fluxus movements, which didn't mean scratch to me and Trevor Thomas. When the dude excused himself, we leaned in and investigated the fliers.

"Wowie zowie," said Trevor Thomas. "Look at this. I could do something like *this*! All I'd need is a picture of Willie Mays. I must have an old card lying around somewhere."

My nose tingled. The fliers were stuck to the wall with rubber cement. "This is almost as good as something you would do," I said, because I too had forgotten that Bring Mays Back was a Trevor Thomas project.

"Hmpf. It's such a pity," he said. "Like all the best ideas are already taken."

Yes, it *was* a pity. I had a tiny sick feeling in my throat. I felt I could cry.

"C'mon, be tough, old boy," he sniffled, putting an arm around my shoulders. "We're letting the rubber cement fumes get the best of us."

§

Another time Trevor Thomas hunkered down at the kitchen table all weekend long with my typewriter. "Privacy," he demanded, shooing me away. "Work in progress." He might have been crafting an epic poem or retyping the phone book for all the noise he was making. And you might think it bothered me, but I was often lonely and glad for the company. Late that first night, he joined me on the loveseat for a spaceship movie starring monkeys with ray guns. "Space apes," he said. "Moon baboons. Har har." And before I could ask what he'd been typing, his head dropped onto the armrest and he was asleep.

He typed the entire next day, pounding the keys and slamming the carriage. By evening my stomach was rumbling. I poked my head into the kitchen to ask if he was hungry. "Now that you say something, I believe I'm on the verge of fainting. I want pizza, and lots of it." He plunked a handful of coins from his jeans pocket onto the table. "Use this," he said. "I found it in your couch."

It was the mother lode—over fifteen dollars! I stretched my shirt into a coin pouch, and he scooped it in. Then I saw his stack of pages beside the typewriter. "What's that?"

"Nothing," he said. "It's not done yet."

"I'm curious," I said, peeking over his shoulder. "What are you writing?"

"Nothing," he said again, dancing around to block my view. "Have some patience, man."

"Read me a page, or a section. The first line—just a single sentence."

"Okay, here's the first line," he said, boxing me out from the typewriter. "'Page one.'"

"Please," I argued. "Be a pal."

"Oh, fine." He grabbed a sheet from the stack and puckered his lips. "Dear *Chronicle* Editor," he intoned. "I am writing re the rumor of a sea monster dwelling in the strait below the Golden Gate Bridge." This monster, as Trevor Thomas described it, was a kraken or a serpent or a demon whale, preventing passage between the Presidio and the Marin Headlands. "As a concerned citizen, I urge you to investigate this matter," he said. "I anticipate a mayoral declaration on whether traversing the bridge is safe. Sincerely yours, Albert Peacock."

"Who's Albert Peacock?"

"I made him up," he said. "And that's just the beginning." His stack of pages was an inch high already, and crumpled sheets lay on the linoleum floor. "Buddy, I'm starving. What about that pizza?"

The next morning I was watching the football pre-game when Trevor Thomas shouted from the kitchen, "Fifty, hot cha!" He stomped in and punched the knob on the television. I pulled my legs underneath me on the loveseat. "Okay," he said, beginning with the Albert Peacock letter. "Dear *Chronicle* Editor." Then letters from Karen Crumbs, Poof

Nunson, Cactus Randall Butts. Time and again—*fifty letters!*—he portrayed what he came to dub the Golden Gate Monster.

"Local sailors report five heads and twenty mouths," read Trevor Thomas. "Scales like razors, fangs like titanium." With each letter, the legend grew. The monster's eyes were acid fire, its tail a snaky lasso. It devoured yachts and rowboats alike, spun tsunamis with a single belch. "Must we never again cross into Marin County? Please, brandish your pens!" Letters scattered the floor. In his hand was the final page. "Most sincerely yours," he said, "Timmy Tumbleweed."

Yes! I was nodding my head like I was listening to music. It was monumental! It was what I should have expected from Trevor Thomas.

He sat next to me on the loveseat. "Niners game on yet?"

The game was just starting, and he conked out at the opening kickoff.

I'm trying to think now if any letters got published, or whether the *Chronicle* ever reported on the Golden Gate Monster. It seems like something I'd remember. What might have happened was that Trevor Thomas didn't have envelopes or postage, then something else captured his fancy and he plumb forgot.

§

There were long stretches when I didn't see Trevor Thomas. He and I went our separate ways at the Art Institute. Previously I'd dabbled in painting and collage, animation, welded sculptures, and décollage, and admittedly I suffered flights of attention. Eventually I homed in on music, composing scores for sine waves and reverb on a four-track recorder.

To create a composition, I would scrape the high string of my bass guitar with a butter knife, then stomp my looping pedal once I'd achieved the desired sine arc. I might alter the tone and pitch by toggling the dials on my four-track, or add trap cadence, Moog sound effects, or an additional bass rhythm. Sometimes I knocked cans around, clapped my shoes together, or imitated wildlife sounds as I imagined them. And when the song reached its crescendo, often dissonant, I stripped the accompaniment layer by layer to arrive back at the original sine wave. Sometimes I forgot to clean the butter knife and made a mess of my bass guitar.

I even cut a tape—*The Best Sogs with Carl Lehmann* (typo my fault)! For a couple years I gigged around the Bay Area, taking sandwiches for pay. And once I sold my five-hundredth and final copy of *Best Sogs*, I called myself happily retired.

With my music, I felt truly in control. And because I knew it would never bring me any money or fame, I pursued my own vision. Those days in San Francisco, self-indulgence was going at a cut rate. Before my wife entered the picture, it was music that kept my head glued on proper.

My wife—she's everything to me! Her name is Betty!

Betty and me are kindred. We're the best of friends. She's always smiling and I'm happy to please her. Her dark hair is cut into a bob, and she has a delicate little nose and cheekbones. One time as a prank, she disconnected the starter in my Subaru and placed a handwritten note under the hood saying I was her spark plug. Another time, I drew her likeness as a constellation and stuck it on our fridge. Betty is the object of all my adoration. I could brag about her until my voice escapes me. How's this for a story: I love my wife!

We live in a suburb of the Twin Cities called Maple Grove. I'm a tax accountant now. Betty works from home selling hospital supplies. We even have a son, a bratty but well-meaning teenager named Carl Jr. Life is a gas! It's constantly wonderful. I couldn't be unhappy if I tried.

Betty and I met when she was waiting tables at a roadside diner in Tucumcari, New Mexico. After I left California, I took work erecting aluminum-sided storage units. Our team of six moved from town to town, pocketing straight cash. I was our concrete man, building plywood forms and handling screed. I got lost in that job. Weeks at a time could pass without my noticing.

In Tucumcari we blew the whistle at sundown and headed to Betty's diner. Immediately I was keen on her. She was a doll and a top-notch waitress to boot. When I special-ordered my burgers with hot mustard and extra coleslaw, she would stop me and wink, saying, "I remember, Mr. Picky." But there was a problem: Betty was pregnant. She was only five-and-a-half feet tall with rail-thin arms and legs, yet she looked as though she was carrying triplets. I cursed my luck that she'd found her man already. It got me down, even. Once Betty left with our orders, I would settle into the mopes. Finally, one of the construction fellas told me to buck up and ask her out.

"It would never work," I conceded. "There's already a luckier man than me."

"Look at her finger, numbnuts." That fella held the back of his hand over the Formica tabletop. "No ring. Open your eyes, numbnuts. She might got one in the oven, but that don't mean some dope's got his gas line screwed in her backside."

All through dinner, my head and heart were in a tizzy. I stayed at the table once the other boys had left. When she came to bus our dishes, I told her my name was Carl.

"Oh," she said.

"Yeah," I said. "What's your name?"

"Betty." She tapped her nametag. "You knew that."

I said it was a pretty name, and with her long black hair she looked nothing like Betty from the Archie comics. We kept talking. Her eyes shined. She smiled and her teeth gleamed. With the fluorescent ring above her, I could be led to believing in angels.

The boys in the pickup honked at me to get moving.

"Say, Betty, maybe you already got some dude," I said, "some dude who treats you right, or maybe your boyfriend, who's probably a righteous fellow—"

"I don't have a boyfriend," she said. "Will you go out with me?"

I said, "Yes!"

That weekend she took me out in Tecumcari, which was her hometown. We went to a honky-tonk and danced, but she kept her distance, red-faced and sweating because of the pregnancy. "Let's rest," she said after a while. We claimed a booth, ordered two root beers, and listened to the fiddle players. "Can I tell you something?" she asked. "You promise you won't run away?"

"Sure," I said. "I promise."

"I'm not really pregnant." She wrinkled her nose, and even that was cute. "It's a foam suit," she said. "So people at the diner will leave bigger tips. Even my boss knows. No one catches on, because all our customers are drifters like you."

"Is there a baby in it?"

"No. It's a suit. It's made of foam."

"You're not pregnant?"

"No, Carl. Here." She pressed my hand against the stomach, then raised her blouse to reveal flesh-colored padding and elastic straps.

"You trickster," I said. "You tricked me! I've been leaving you thirty percent."

She grinned like a kitten to milk. Then I unfastened her suit and tossed it under the table, and we cut it up on the dance floor until long after the musicians had left the stage.

In time we got married and I made Betty pregnant for real. But it wasn't until her third trimester that I remembered that old suit. Suddenly I was on deadline to cook up a snappy joke. When we were driving home after a Twins game, she told me her water had broke.

"Nice try, Betty. You've been playing this game ever since we met."

"Carl, get in the left lane. We need to go to the hospital. Left lane, Carl."

"Fool me once," I said.

"Carl, change lanes. Now! Change lanes, Carl. You're going home, but we need the hospital. Carl! Change! Lanes! Listen to me!"

"Uh-huh. Do me a favor, Betty." I looked into her eyes. "Bring me my mustard burger and coleslaw on the double." Then I swung the wheel for the ramp toward the hospital. I looked at her again, and she was smiling. I tricked her!

§

I did poorly at the Art Institute. After a while, I knew it was senseless to continue. For several months I was unemployed and without purpose. Often I found myself parked on the loveseat, my mind drifting to the image of a golden eagle with the head of an alligator.

How could such a bird exist? You could replace an alligator's front legs with wings, then shorten its body to reduce drag. Its head would be tall and feathery, with a gaping snout and lizard eyes. Only the redwoods at Big Sur would be worthy of such majesty. And the bird was benevolent—a pacifist, maybe even a vegetarian. There on the trails, it protected day-hikers from bears, mountain lions, and perverts. And for its name, of course: the eaglegator.

Thoughts of the eaglegator were bouncing around my skull one afternoon when Trevor Thomas barged in with a sack of oranges and a bag of ice. "Hey champ, I need to use your blender," he said. "Do you have a blender?"

I shook my head no, absently.

"Ground control to Major Tom. What's going on, space cadet?"

"Do you have a minute?" I said. "I've been having some serious thoughts lately … about a mythical bird."

He set down his bags and sat cross-legged on the floor, like a kid at story hour.

"To start," I said, "imagine an alligator egg washing up into an eagle nest. Then imagine the mother eagle raising it as her own." This child was different from his siblings, swampy in hues, heavy with spines and scales. He fluttered clumsily in flight and botched his landings. Awkward and maligned, he was neither this nor that. Then one day a coastal storm hit the forest, washing through the trees and destroying the family's nests. The eagles bawled and piped. Yet with his strong talons, the eaglegator built new nests of the sturdiest logs, and with his great jaw he collected nuts and berries to feed his clan. He gained a sense—if not of belonging—then of contributing. He was unique, as we all are, and he accepted his difference as a virtue.

"Yes," said Trevor Thomas, bouncing his knees like a seesaw. "The eaglegator! I can see it now. He can fly underwater, he can swim in the air."

"Well, I never said that."

"He flaps his wings to make monsoons and stop all the forest fires."

"Hmm," I said. "I hadn't considered that."

Trevor Thomas wanted to know more. Was there an archenemy? What was the creature's wingspan? Did it speak English? Mexican? Bear language? What about lasers? Is the eaglegator immortal?

"Your ice is melting all over the floor."

"Oh, nuts!" he said, jumping to his feet. "Gotta go." He thumped an index finger against his temple. "Good thinking, Carl. Love it."

I soon forgot about the eaglegator. After I left the Institute, my federal loans got rescinded. To make ends meet, I pawned my Moog and four-track and took work as a landscaping grunt. The job was humiliating. My nose went pink with sunburn, I was always hungry, and the boys on the crew would burp out vulgarities and chuck dirt at each other's crotches for a joke. In the evenings I returned home covered in earth and fell straight to sleep without bathing.

One night Trevor Thomas was waiting outside on my stoop.

"Good news, old boy!"

"I'm in the mood for good news," I said, unlocking the door. As was usual during this stretch, I was tired and regrettably irritable, and only wanted to collapse onto my loveseat. "You don't mind if I sit, do you? I'm pooped."

"Please do," he said. "Get comfortable. We're gonna take a quiz."

"No!"

"First question: What is the nickname of San Francisco's pro football team?"

"Forty-Niners," I said, kicking off my boots.

"Why are they called the Forty-Niners?"

"Gold Rush of 1849."

"Lastly, what does a Forty-Niner look like?" Before I could muster a guess, he handed me a sheet of paper from his back pocket. "This, my friend, is the new-look Forty-Niners."

The paper was a lithograph facsimile. Three lines curved upward in a half-circle. Below that was a silhouette of rugged mountains. And flying between them was a caricature I knew immediately to be the eaglegator. It was pretty much how I'd described him, except his eyes were bulgy and disgustingly garish.

I shoved the paper at Trevor Thomas.

He shoved it back at me.

"I'll explain," he said, plopping down on the loveseat. "These three lines: one for Trevor Thomas, one for Carl Lehmann, one for the eaglegator. They'll run down the middle of the helmet. Then the side logos will be the mountains and the beast."

"He's not a beast."

"Imagine it," said Trevor Thomas, billboarding with his hands, "wings of an eagle, teeth of a gator, all them little babies serving pancakes on the offensive line. But listen, we need to spread the myth. I'll storyboard a comic book, and you can write the words. *Birth of the Eaglegator*. You with me, Carl? I told the suits at Candlestick I'd have a mockup by next week."

"No," I moaned. "Did you send this out?"

He pointed to the letterhead: PARTNERSHIP OF TREVOR & CARL.

"Why you looking at me like that? I ordered three boxes of this stationery. I thought you'd be tickled."

I was not tickled. I felt betrayed. The eaglegator had been my private creation, and I demanded he drop the idea. But no, he refused. We were doing a public service, he claimed, since no one knew what a Forty-Niner looked like or whether it even existed. "But soon everyone—" he said, "everyone will know the eaglegator beast."

"Quit calling him a beast," I snapped. "The eaglegator is friendly. He's kind and cooperative. In his heart, he's trying to find where he belongs."

"But you can't have a softie for a mascot," said Trevor Thomas, snatching the paper from my hands. "We'll compromise: he'll look dangerous as heck, but he'll be on the helmets, which keep players safe."

"Darnit, Trevor, you're not listening!" I picked up a boot and slammed the heel on the floor. "That's not the eaglegator I know. You take my name off!"

He quit pacing the room. "Fine, I'll take your name off." He tore the CARL from the letterhead and dropped it to the floor. "The idea's mine now."

"Good. Leave me alone, Trevor Thomas."

"Happily," he said, stuffing the sheet in his back pocket. "So long, Carl. You're being a butthole." And he stormed out, slamming the door behind himself.

That's where things ended, the talk of the eaglegator and my friendship with Trevor Thomas. At my worst, I posted a sign on my door that read, NO TREVOR THOMASES'S ALLOWED. Neither of us were ones to hold a grudge, but he never returned, even once I removed the sign.

§

I don't recall any singular incident that made me leave San Francisco. It was just one of those feelings in my gut. Everything changed, and nothing was familiar. Among other things, my mother, who was eighty years old and living in a nursing home back in Alameda, passed away. She'd had me while in her fifties. My two older brothers and my sister were separated from me by twenty years. Except for my sister, who'd coddled me while I was young but then disappeared and cut off contact, my siblings and I never knew each other. With my mother gone, I realized I was alone in California, maybe alone in the world.

I left town without saying goodbye to anyone. Just one night I was gone, no explanation given. How could I have done that? If I remember correctly, my lease had expired, which at the time seemed as good a reason as any.

§

Why am I thinking about all this now? Because last week Debbie Beecham sent me an email saying Trevor Thomas had become killed in a boating accident on San Francisco Bay.

I found this entirely shocking. I had forgotten about Trevor Thomas. His whereabouts and whatabouts had eluded me. But also, I didn't know who Debbie Beecham was or how she got my email address. Because I believed the whole thing to be a joke, I printed the message to take home and show Betty. But I kept forgetting it in my briefcase. It wasn't until Betty was packing my lunch last Friday that she finally asked about Debbie Beecham's message. I said I was hoping she could tell me.

"Debbie's that woman from the farmers' market," she said. "You remember your spat at the dunking booth."

This I did remember. Last fall, Betty and I stuck Carl Jr. on a Boy Scout trip and drove down to Rochester for a farmers' market. It was a big gathering, more like a fair. As we were walking the midway, a man called to me from the seat of a Lions Club dunking booth. "Hey featherweight, with the purty wife. Let's see that arm, sally." His words struck me as rude, and in a fit of pride I bought three softballs from the ticket woman. It was a bad idea. The man heckled me mercilessly, for I'd never been taught to throw. After my second ball arced high over the target, he cackled, "Try it underhand, nancy."

"You watch your mouth," I shouted back.

We traded a series of unkind words, to the point where I refused to throw the final softball. It became a serious tiff. Several lookyloos stopped to check on the fuss.

Betty pulled me aside and told me to cool it, mister, when a lady in a pantsuit said, "Carl? Carl Lehmann?" It was Debbie Beecham, though I didn't recognize her. She introduced herself and explained to Betty how she and I had been friends back in San Francisco. Yes, Debbie Beecham! Back then her tangled hair reached down to her waist and her bead jewelry clicked with every motion. Now here we were, both in our fifties at a farmers' market in Nowheresville, U.S.A., and I had just narrowly avoided a scuffle.

"We lost touch once you left San Francisco," said Debbie Beecham. "It was like one day you just vanished."

"This is true," I said.

"So what's become of you, Carl? How have you been?"

Well, I said, things are pretty darn good. Betty and me have lived in the Twin Cities almost twenty years now. We are happy, healthy, and lucky. Property values are up, mortgage rates are down. We have a kid we enroll in all sorts of clubs and lessons so he doesn't pester us every minute of the day. Betty was running for School Board, and I'd become quite the ace at badminton. My joints and hairline are that of a teenager. No complaints here! Life, as I explained it, was a simple and satisfying matter.

So that was Debbie Beecham. But then, while packing my lunch, Betty asked about Trevor Thomas. I had to leave for work, so I kissed her goodbye and promised we would talk that night.

But how was I to explain about Trevor Thomas? Believe it or not, Betty and I had hardly discussed our respective pasts. With her, I started anew. And how could I narrate my history when the details are so jumbled in my own mind? These memories, you blink and they're gone! Even the mementos—the fliers, letters, and glitter—they're probably scattered with the wind, blowing gradually into the bay. Or of the *Best Sogs* cassettes, I'd be lucky if even one isn't smashed up and forgotten. If only I had a copy, I would crank the volume high and say, Betty, my love, this here's a tune from California Carl.

When I returned home that night, Betty met me in the kitchen and took my briefcase. "Hey mister," she said, "you look like you're in a cloud. What gives?"

"I had a crummy day," I said. "My focus was out the window."

"Oh, Carl." She put a hand on my arm. "Take your time. We have all weekend."

This was right! We'd sent Carl Jr. to a math camp or a swimming meet, and the weekend was mine and Betty's.

"I want to tell you everything," I said, "but I don't know how to say it."

She waited for me.

"Trevor Thomas was a guy I used to be friends with."

"I know. I spoke with Debbie this afternoon."

She and I made cocoa and went out into the den. We sat beside each other on the sofa, and she told me about her phone call with Debbie Beecham.

Trevor Thomas had been booted from the Art Institute, after which he took odd jobs painting houses and moving office equipment, laying down the yellow stripes on the highway. Nothing seemed to stick. He grappled with panic and despair, and to combat these feelings he would set out fishing on a secondhand pontoon. He didn't mind going it alone. One day he was out off Gashouse Cove and something happened, a gust of wind, or he fell asleep. No one's sure. There was no foul play, no drugs or alcohol. And Trevor Thomas had hardly anyone in his life when he passed. He's buried up in Marin County in a plot beside his parents, who'd apparently been gone as long as I'd known him.

I think about death sometimes, though I don't discuss it with Betty. And I think it's only like going to sleep: your eyelids droop, you might snort or kick your legs, then before you know, you've faded into dreams. The end. But for Trevor Thomas, who drowned, it must have been like a party with everyone you know and trust, where everything's familiar and you feel safe. You let loose, finding your rhythm, until you notice it's early and you've been overdoing it, and unless you turn back now, you're facing the blackout. Yet you think, *I've done this before, I know my limits*, and what started as a shade of gray becomes total black pitch darkness.

"Debbie said you played guitar," Betty said.

"I played bass guitar. Some other things too."

She clasped my hand there on the sofa.

"What did Trevor play?"

"I don't remember him being into music," I said. "But he was keen at lithographs and drawing. He was an idea man." Betty nodded for me to continue. "Trevor Thomas lived behind me in the Mission District. You could never predict when he'd appear. And his ideas, they'd blow your hair back."

I went on. One story led to the next—Minty Coke, Bring Mays Back, the Golden Gate Monster, and that whole stink over the eaglegator. Soon I was on my feet, acting out scenes and putting on voices. Betty pulled her legs up underneath herself. "Slow down, Carl," she said. "You're rattling on so fast I can't keep up." But I'd been set loose like a whirlwind, rambling forward, my mouth hardly keeping pace with my mind. Shadows rolled across the den, until the sky outside turned dark with night.

When I finally dropped back onto the sofa, Betty leaned into me and said, "I wish I had a chance to know Trevor." Yes, I said, he made himself known. And I had the urge to keep talking, to keep on telling stories. But I couldn't think of any I hadn't just told her.

I know there's more!

(CAN YOU SWIM?)

You might find yourself at a riverbank after dark. No moon, no stars, only the breeze shuffling cattails on the flats. Wild grasses brush your legs, mud pierces the gaps between your toes. Behind you is an industrial hum: crickets perhaps, or locusts. The faint, far-off scents of cedar and pine. Then on the opposite bank you see a blinking amber light. It flashes steadily and with measure, in rhythm with a heartbeat, maybe your own. The light is large, hundreds of yards away. Or else it's smaller, much closer. Something passes with the current—driftwood, the trunk of a fallen tree. You're probably lost to have come upon this river. And you must be curious about the amber light. It's there beyond the riverbed, flashing through the darkness, unerring.

ROAD SONGS

When we were sophomores, a boy from school named Jason Fleury got his forearm tattooed in big gothic letters saying MY OWN MAN. Not knowing what else to do, the vice-principal sent him home for the week and suspended him from the basketball team, like that would change anything. Fleury was a friend of mine, though he's not important to this story. He was a Dakota Sioux boy whose father appeared only once or twice a year, always feisty and quarrelsome. Fleury told me about it in the lunchroom and the parking lot—mean, dispiriting stories. You wondered how a kid like that would ever escape such a pattern of anguish. Choosing a mantra and tattooing it on his body, I suppose. And hearing his stories, I decided an absent father seemed not such a bad thing, so long as he remained absent.

At the time, I hadn't much thought of my father or even imagined his existence. He and my mother never married, and he was so long gone that asking questions was pointless. I would later learn that he'd been a baseball prospect, a touring musician, and a rodeo man, stirring dust all across the Great Plains. He was, by all accounts, a man of great promise.

So I was raised by my mother, a nurse. We lived on the south end of Aberdeen, a former railway hub near the James River of South Dakota. It was the town where my mother was raised, and her mother before her. We had even lived with my grandmother at first. Back then, my mother worked doubles and overnights until she could purchase us our own house, which was simple and modest, and our lives then were indeed modest. I remember those days in that small house with my mother as contented times.

Though when she turned thirty-five, as she recently had on this day I'm describing, my mother began to drift. She could be impassive or despondent—*dreamy*, the word might be. Many nights I lay awake after dark when the front door would unlatch and I'd know that I was alone. Where had she gone? My mother was not a drinker, nor a user, nor one who craves the attention or affection of others. No, on these nights she was only walking, observing the same old neighborhoods she'd known for so many years. Elsewhere, she might have imagined, my father was leading a romantic life, one of freedom and opportunity.

The truth, however, is not romantic. My father had chances, yes, but he squandered them. He drank and fought, fled town on a whim, worked cash-in-hand jobs running cattle and raising steel structures. Then somewhere in Kansas, he saw a foreman die beneath the boom of a crane my father himself was operating. Up around Sioux City, he wrecked a company vehicle in a one-car accident. In Billings, he met a flight attendant and had a young daughter—my half-sister—who died in a creek at age six. And in the face of all these miseries, he took work driving big rigs and found himself there, unattached as he'd always been, unfettered and unloosed.

§

He was in this particular state one late-winter morning when he introduced himself into my life. This was March of my sophomore year. It was track season, and on this morning I'd gone out training on my own. The night before, we'd gotten one of those damp, heavy snowfalls, and the streets were soupy with slush. When I returned home he was there, my father, sitting by himself at our kitchen table. "Hello, Scotty," said my mother from beside the stove. "How was your run? This here is Rick Lohse."

Just then I didn't know Rick Lohse from a stranger on the side of the road. He was a handsome man with whitish-blond hair and a childish face. If not for how he was dressed—leather boots and worn-in jeans, denim jacket with a white fleece collar—I might have thought he was a military recruiter or someone making a church call.

"I forgot to say Rick was coming," said my mother, bringing me a glass of water from the sink. "Rick travels."

"I'm passing through," he said, standing up and offering his hand. "Hi, Scotty."

"Hello, sir," I said.

"*Sir?*" my mother laughed. "Sit down, you two, and I'll *serve* you some breakfast."

The table had been set in my absence. As I've said already, our house was modest and our furnishings too. But for this occasion, my mother had brought out the woven placemats and earthen stoneware. I took a seat beside Rick Lohse, and she carried over eggs and sausage, potatoes, melon and blueberries, buttered toast—an uncommon feast.

"You didn't answer the question," said Rick. "How was your run, Scotty?"

"Fine," I said.

"Just fine?"

"It was good," I said. "It's messy out there, and my socks got wet. But it was good. I took the bike trail out around Wylie Park and back." Rick showed disbelief—that must be eight miles, he said. "Actually, I think it's more like ten," I said.

"Well, your mother says you're fast. She tell you I was a runner too?"

"No, sir, I didn't know that."

"You can lay off the 'sir' business," he said. "*Rick* is fine."

"Okay, Rick," I said.

My mother joined us at the table. She and I were not a praying family, and we passed around the dishes and began to eat. At this age, I was always hungry. I filled my plate and hung on the periphery of the conversation. Rick was a long-haul trucker. That's why he'd come through town this morning. He said in the past week alone he'd been from Wenatchee to Winnipeg, but I cared very little and didn't respond. Now he was en route to Colorado, moving a load of Amish furniture to a wholesaler there.

"A load of what?" said my mother. "Do you pick these things, or they pick you?"

"I can choose," said Rick. "But I ain't the type to turn down work."

"You never did sit still," my mother said.

"I like to move. That's true."

Here he went into a brief soliloquy about life on the road, making it out to be an adventure and a privilege. I was drinking juice and reaching for dishes, paying only half-attention. No, driving truck wasn't the life he'd imagined, he said, the road was lonesome and long, but it was always changing. You had turnouts and toll booths, two-lane asphalt and wide-open freeways. To be honest, he sounded pompous like a salesman, and he must have known he'd gotten too serious. "Oh, wait," he said, searching the table. "Am I missing something? I'm looking for the lefse roll-ups."

My mother grinned. "This is not a holiday, Rick."

The lefse was a reference I only caught halfway. Lefse was Norwegian flatbread, a potato crepe my grandmother served with butter and sugar when we gathered as a family.

"And how is Mira?" Rick said. "I'm supposing she never asks about me."

"If she ever mentioned your name, it would not be in spirit of the holidays."

What world was this? I felt like I'd wandered into a stage play without having rehearsed my lines, perhaps into a scene I didn't even belong. Mirabelle was my grandmother, though no one called her

Mira. Rick was teasing—you could tell by his sly nature—and my mother said she was fine, my grandmother, that she still bowled in a league and golfed with the Rotarians. She might live to one hundred, my mother said, maybe longer.

"And how about you, Franny? What do you do these days for fun?"

"For *fun*?" She laughed at the question. "Why, it's all pretty fun, isn't it, Scotty? Every day is a gas in this house. Fun isn't something we add to the schedule."

"Now that's the attitude."

"Driving fast and serenading girls," said my mother. "That's one idea of fun."

It was then I recognized him as my father. I could tell by the intimacy between him and my mother and the history it implied. Certainly, I was expected to know this already. And thinking about it then, even his name was familiar. I believed I had once taken a phone message from Rick Lohse. I set down my fork and napkin—I wasn't sick or upset or even all that surprised. I just needed a moment for my thoughts to catch up with the others at the table.

"Scotty, are you finished?" my mother said. "You look cold. Maybe you should change out of your running clothes."

"I am cold," I said. "I might take a shower."

"Go ahead. Afterward, Rick says he's giving us a piano recital."

"I did not say 'recital,'" he said. "That was your word, Franny."

"No one calls her Franny anymore," I said, but my tone was rude and I'd stood up too suddenly. I placed my hand on the chair for balance. "Excuse me," I added, and thanked my mother for breakfast.

§

Rick was not a good piano player. When I got to the living room, he was plunking his way through "Für Elise," a music-box tune if there ever was one. He would halt and repeat phrases, hum the tune and replicate it without success. "I should confess," he said. "I'm out of form. Your mother talked me into this."

"We call that false modesty," she said. "Or a premature excuse."

I sat beside her on the couch, at a side angle to the piano. Rick turned his efforts to "Camptown Races," a song I could have played with even five minutes of instruction. And then, of all the elementary songs, he tapped out the melody for "Happy Birthday to You."

"Ha ha," said my mother. "The number-one hit."

"I'm warming up. Feel free to sing along."

"Oh, but now we've forgotten the words."

He abruptly stood. He produced a penlight from his jacket, folded back the top board, and peered into the cabinet of the piano. "This thing is poorly out of tune," he said, and he had a point. For all I knew the piano had come with the house, and it served now as little more than a bureau table and a place to stack our mail. Rick strummed the wires, which made a jagged harp-like sound. "Hammers are all grooved out. These wires are rusty."

"Right," said my mother. "One might suggest that you, in fact, are the rusty one."

"Fran, you got a hex key? These tuning pins are so loose."

"Hex key? Probably out in the shed." She looked at me, but I hardly knew a hex key from a vise grip. "I'll get it," she said. "You keep Amadeus here company."

It was afternoon now, and sunlight shone through the south-facing windows. Once my mother left, Rick got to his feet and studied the walls. I saw what was coming, and I hoped to avoid it. On the walls were a dozen landscape drawings of mine, done with charcoal pencils and drafting paper. Much to my embarrassment, my mother had hung them there like museum pieces.

"Who's the artist here?" Rick asked.

"That would be me," I said. "Those drawings are kind of old."

"Look at the variety of these trees … the shading in this valley."

I was very good at drawing. This was true. For a time I even thought I would illustrate comic books, but drawing felt juvenile to me now. My problem was that I lacked imagination. My sketches were rich with detail and precise in scale, but they were mere facsimiles. "Those are copies," I said. "Mom brings home issues of *Outdoor Life* and *National Geographic* from the hospital. They're not original, so to speak. I don't really draw anymore."

"Now you run."

"That's right."

He settled back down at the piano bench. "And you're quite the runner?"

"I do well," I said. He waited for me to continue. "I run the mile and two-mile, and the relays. Last year I was anchor on our medley relay team that got runner-up at state. We were in sixth when I got the baton, and we rallied to within meters of winning it all."

"*We?*"

"I rallied," I said. "I'm quick. This year I'm gonna break the school record in the mile."

Rick had been testing the black keys, but now he stopped.

"That's funny. I used to have that record. Four thirty-five."

I was quiet a moment. And then it clicked: that was how I knew the name Rick Lohse. "You still have the record," I said. "Your name is still up on the gymnasium wall."

He smiled—a prideful, crooked smile. Rick Lohse was a prideful man. I would come to know that smile, that of a conniver or an egotist, one whose charm both allures and bewitches. "Is that right?" he said. "Goddamn. Well, I'm glad we ain't racing today."

"You wouldn't stand a chance in those pointy boots."

He laughed at that and played a ragtime scale. Then he leaned forward and placed his chin in his hand. "Tell me, Scotty. You ever wonder what goes on outside this town? You probably been in Aberdeen your whole life."

"I travel for sports."

"That's local. You know, there's a big world out there. Like I'm hauling this furniture down to Colorado, and then I'm coming back this way. I've driven those roads a hundred times, but you never seen them, and you might be curious. All these landscapes," he said, pointing at my drawings, "and you're copying them from magazines."

I wasn't sure what he meant. I was only sixteen—how far should I have gone? And the way he'd said it was like an invitation. Before I could make a response, my mother returned with what I'd call Allen wrenches.

"That's one less excuse," she said, handing them to Rick. "Any more delays and we'll start asking for refunds."

He took out his penlight again and leaned over the cabinet. The work was mysterious and slow, but when he tested the keys you could hear the difference. Nonetheless, it was a tedious process. My mother clapped her hands and said to quit stalling. "Do you want melody," he said, "or do you want a tin can pushed down a meat grinder? All right, last one." He closed the cabinet and took his seat, raised his chin, straightened his back, and set his legs to ninety degrees. His posture was like that of a concert pianist. And then deftly, decisively, he struck a lower-octave chord and became someone else entirely.

The song he played began dark and moody. It was a modern piece, supple like jazz. His left hand pounded chords while his right played sparingly the grace notes. The song was pretty, but it was repetitive. He was holding back, groping for the rhythm, like finding his way through an unlit room. And just when you thought he was stuck, he crossed his hands and the notes swelled, and the music whistled off like a bottle rocket.

Now he was *playing*. I couldn't say if it was a waltz or a hymn or a polonaise—it just sounded *good*. To hear those notes was to feel the warmth and the promise of spring. I looked outside just as a clump of snow dropped from the trees.

"Do you like train songs?" he said over his shoulder. "How about road songs?"

"Shut up and keep playing!" said my mother.

The couch was shaking. She was bouncing her foot.

Rick swayed at the bench. He had verve, and he had soul. His boots were lithe over the pedals. "I grew up with my face in a road map, until I took to the trail like a dart," he sang. "I got no steady address, they call me Pony Express, and my rig is the wild, wild heart."

These were major-key songs, lively and grand. They moved like wind through a tunnel or water around rocks—you got swept with the current. He created sounds I didn't know could be extracted from those keys. And he was a showman, splicing in frills and trills, playing to the crowd. It went on. And when later he found again that original phrase, the darker one, he repeated it softly and more slowly, until he released the foot pedal and left the absence of notes, a stillness more profound for the music that had come before.

"That's called 'Hometown Medley.' I just made it up."

"Bullshit," crowed my mother.

"Yeah, those were the old songs in no particular order."

I was no longer in the room. I was somewhere else, hiding or floating above. I *was* there, but I had no reason to be and felt invisible. Beside me, my mother's face was flushed and she held her hands to her cheeks. Rick rotated his arm and cracked his shoulder, then he closed the lid over the keys.

§

My mother asked me to put on more coffee. She and Rick went out into the yard. She wanted to show him the garden plot, the shed, our one lilac tree that would soon come into bloom. I cleared away the dishes and wrapped the extra food, and by then they still weren't back. Outside, the door to the shed was closed and its window glazed over. And when the coffee finished bubbling, I quit sitting around the kitchen table by myself.

An odd thought had taken hold of me: that my father's way of life was something to be admired, perhaps even envied. The idea seared into my nerves, and in my bedroom I packed a gym bag with a few shirts and a pair of pants, socks and underwear, seventy-five dollars from under my mattress—enough to last me, I guessed, three days on the road.

Rick's truck was parked one street over, an eighteen-wheeler with a muscular cab and a straight box trailer. The plates were from Nevada, but it had to be Rick's truck. Eighteen-wheelers didn't come through our part of town. The trailer was grimy from weather, marked with the word TRANSPORTS. I hoisted myself up by a handlebar and found the driver-side door unlocked.

The cabin had two bucket seats with a gear shift between them. Everything was vinyl, cream and tan, and the dashboard was like mission control with all its switches and dials and analog screens. There was a ball compass and a CB radio, cubbies stuffed with tie-downs and tools, batteries, pipe cleaners, carbon paper, duct tape and electrical tape. The cabin was clean. It was tidy and bright, well-manicured like Rick himself. Except for the ashtray, which was stuffed with wooden cigar tips, you'd think a maid had been through only an hour before.

Behind the seats was a carpeted partition, which opened to a cot and clothing locker, storage totes, even a toaster oven and a small refrigerator. A man could *live* here, I thought, and perhaps Rick did. I set my bag on the floor and caught my reflection in a mirror. It was bordered with vanity lights, and on the shelf below was an open tube of concealer.

Back inside, my mother and Rick were again at the kitchen table. I startled them when I came through the front door. "Oh, hello again," said my mother. "Were you outside?"

"Yes," I said. "I went to the truck."

"The truck?" Rick said.

"I took my bag out."

"What?"

He and I looked at my mother. Her fingers were braided over her coffee mug, and she'd turned her head like she was listening for something far away. She was drifting, I could see it. "Me and him are going to Colorado," I said. "We'll call you from the road. Maybe I can buy a camera and take pictures." My thoughts were way out ahead of me, but there was no reining them in. "Mom, will you call the school and excuse me? Tell my coach we'll be back in a few days."

"That's fine," she quietly said.

Rick was worrying the collar of his denim jacket. "Scotty, are you sure?"

"I already decided."

"Franny?"

But my mother was then unreachable. She'd gone dreamy—you could tell by the distance in her eyes. She was seeing through me, or past me, onto the slush in the streets or a patch of brown lawn. "We're leaving now, Mom. This'll be okay," I said. "Mom, are you listening?"

§

Rick and I headed west on a two-lane highway while the sky was still cloudless and blue. We passed by farmhouses and muddy fields, small ponds on which the ice was receding. Rick steered with a spinner knob on the wheel, which lay almost parallel to his lap. The CB radio crackled on with coded, taciturn messages, background noise like a birdcall in sunlight.

I asked what was so special about Amish furniture. The craftsmanship, Rick said. It's built to last. Was it always furniture in back? No, he said, he was a contract driver. He'd driven grain trucks and hauled cattle, timber, lumber, granite slabs. He was not a corporate driver, though he'd moved new cars and heavy machinery, turbine blades and fifty-foot augers. "This is only temporary," he said. "Driving truck is not my forever career."

He asked if I played baseball. He said he'd played shortstop for a Single-A team in Wisconsin Rapids, and in only half a season he'd set the league record for inside-the-park home runs. "That's not an official record," he clarified. "They weren't tracking it back then." He said if the ball even touched the outfield grass, he could stretch it into a double. Then the week before he was set for promotion, a guy named Rincon slid hard into second trying to bust up a double play, snapping Rick's ankle. "And that ended that," he said. "I was a contact hitter. Speed was my game." But not for a minute did he believe this Rincon character was playing fair. "These boys will mow you down just to level the field, remember that."

After that he toured with Paulie Knox and the Best Boys, a rockabilly band as he described it. Rick handled keyboards and steel guitar, even sang backing vocals. He and the boys played beer joints, street dances, county fairs. "We'd set up in an empty lot and have a hundred people dancing by dusk." They'd even met Bon Jovi in the early days, and everyone said it was a coin flip which band would break out first.

"I never heard of Paulie Knox," I said.

"You can forget Paulie Knox. The man was a rodent."

"What did he do?"

"Tell you what he didn't do," Rick said. "He didn't write the music *or* the lyrics."

The band's claim to fame—passing fame—was a series of regional anthems all meant for specific radio markets: "Smokin' in Spokane," "Little Miss Missoula," "The Boys from Boise." He sang me a chorus, which was catchy but unfamiliar. The songs weren't meant to be silver records, he said, but some of them sold almost five-thousand copies. "Fort Collins, Provo, Reno, Coeur d'Alene … I could draw you a highway map of the royalties I rightly deserve."

Then there was a rodeo league. Rick himself was not a cowboy, but he was a founding board member and managed all the franchising—venues, sponsorships, licensing. "I took every photo on those trading cards," he said. The league competed on Fridays in the fall, with rosters from Alberta to Oklahoma. "Well, not Oklahoma. But we were getting there. It was in the plans." By year three they'd nearly cleared their debt, but then an old cattleman named Butch Wagner forced Rick out in a power grab and the league soon folded. "Their loss. I was this close," he said, showing with his thumb and forefinger, "*this close* to selling the TV rights. Now we'll never know."

By then the sun had fallen over the western plains. The night had turned dark, starless and moonless. We'd been through Pierre and across the river, through Fort Pierre, further south. We rolled over buttes and bluffs, past icy lakes and penned-in cattle.

"Well, well," Rick said. "Look at this."

He flashed the high beams. Out ahead, a line of white-tailed deer had blockaded the road. There were a half-dozen of them at least, standing still as lawn ornaments, their neon eyes glowing in the lights.

"Slow down," I said. "Rick, stop!"

But he only drifted toward the center line. He pulled the horn and flashed his lights. And in the moment before impact, in the time it would take to snap one's fingers, the deer split like a parting river, their cottony tails bobbing into the ditch. I looked back through the side-view mirror but saw only the running lights of our trailer.

"Fucking crap," I said.

"They know better than we do," said Rick. "They ain't stupid."

"Sure looked that way."

"I been doing this a while," he said.

We turned west onto the interstate. Rick cracked his window and lit a thin cigar. The radio was tuned to a livestock report, with talk of steers and heifers, hogs and poultry. Our headlights shone on billboards and fenceposts, long fields of native grass.

"Do you think you and Mom will ever be a couple again?"

Who said that? I must have said it. But it was a naïve thought that shouldn't have been put to words. Rick cocked his head like he'd misheard me. Ahead of us, an old sedan on the shoulder was flashing its hazards, and we passed it without slowing down. The AM radio crackled, blurring the space between me and Rick.

§

We spent that night at a motel outside Rapid City. The room smelled like ammonia, and its queen-size bed sagged in the middle. "This will not do," Rick said, turning the switch on a lamp to no effect. "I'll be in the cab. You know," he added, "I'm not in the habit of spending money on motels. I'm not upset, I'm just saying."

"I told you I'd sleep in the truck. I'll even pay for the room, I said that."

"No, I insisted, didn't I?"

"You have all that furniture in the trailer. I'd sleep there, it's all the same to me."

"Hmm." He'd been searching the bureau drawers. "That's actually a good goddamn idea, Scotty. But no, this'll work. It's all right. Besides, you need space to stretch them running legs."

"That's fine," I said, lying down on the covers. "Wake me in the morning."

"Early rise," he said, the door slamming shut behind him.

§

The next day we stopped only twice and reached a town called Trinidad with daylight to spare. Rick drove to a warehouse beside the interstate, backed against a loading dock, and jumped down from the cab without a word.

We were in an industrial zone, all concrete and cyclone fencing. Beyond that were dusty flats and then mountains, or just one mountain, I couldn't tell. That afternoon a thick, funereal fog had dropped a ceiling over the highways, and Rick and I had turned inward, saying little. I was glad to be out of the cab. I walked out and pissed through the fence onto a scrubby field.

"What now?" I said, back at the loading dock.

"These boys will unload the truck," Rick said. "I'm gonna file papers and smoke a cigar." He was standing with a clipboard beneath an overhead door. The scent of mildew came from a nearby dumping area—bundled cardboard and sun-faded mattresses.

"I'll help the boys unload."

"No, it's their job."

"Do you need me for anything?" I said. "I might go for a run."

"No, don't do that."

"How come?

"Because what are you trying to do," he said, "break someone's record?"

That was the Rick Lohse charm. He had me off-balance and set me immediately straight. His smile was mischievous, his eyes untelling. He was a calculating man, impossible to predict. He reached out and rustled my hair, our first contact since shaking hands the previous morning.

I changed into my running clothes and took a frontage road into town, no map or directions. The streets of Trinidad were easy enough to navigate. I ran up and over, down and back, along red-brick roads and asphalt with no curbs. Running here was different from running back home: the ground sloped and the air was thinner. I ran uphill and my thighs burned, I went for speed and my lungs felt clamped. But it was just a different sort of workout, except these vistas were new and it took restraint to pace myself.

It's many years later now, and I can still imagine that town with the clarity of a home movie. Running does that for me. It impresses in my mind all the patterns and nuance of the world outdoors—the rhythm of water and the quality of air, the length of shadows. Running releases me, transforms me into something dynamic. I am dust, I am litter. These are not unproductive thoughts. And I become new each time I run, because the act itself is elemental. That afternoon in Trinidad, I easily reconciled my attitudes toward Rick. He was difficult and inconsistent, but here we were and I couldn't change that. Best to breathe and ride it out. He and I might never know one another, though given time we might demonstrate our tolerance and care. I ran for maybe ninety minutes, and when I returned the truck was gone.

"Have you seen my dad?" I asked two men smoking beside the loading dock.

"Who's your dad?" one said.

"I've been running," I said. "I'm sort of tired. Can I sit on these mattresses?"

"They might be wet," said one of the men.

I sat down and loosened my shoes. The men went back inside. Would they be talking to someone about me? It seemed unlikely. I was just a kid in the wrong place. Or I was in the right place—I wasn't confused about that—though I had no idea about my geography and didn't know what should happen next. My brow and cheeks were crusty with sweat. Forklifts beeped from within the warehouse, and the air smelled of pine and gasoline.

I fell asleep. When I woke up, I was very cold. The mattresses were indeed damp.

To the north, city lights cast an aura in the fog. I was so groggy I felt like I'd been drugged—it must have been the altitude. Had everyone else gone home? Was I fenced in? My mind sprinted away from me. Suddenly I was hitchhiking and riding with strangers, or I was sneaking into a church, rummaging for food. I was waving down a policeman, trying not to cry. Collect-calling my mother, and when she didn't answer, my grandmother.

I wasn't alone with these thoughts for long. No sooner than I'd stood up and begun wringing out my shorts, a pair of headlights swept around the warehouse. Rick's truck stopped thirty feet before me, the brakes squealing like a rope being tightened.

"Bucko," he called out. "There's a change in plans."

"Holy shit, I'm glad to see you," I said.

"Where's your pants?"

"It's wet," I said, pointing to a mattress. "It was wet already. It's been rained on."

"We have other concerns."

"I didn't piss myself," I said.

He stepped down with my gym bag. As I got changed, he told me a call had been placed and he'd been rerouted to Huntsville. That's why he'd gone away—he was down the highway loading pallets of engine parts into the trailer. "This was not my choice," he said. "These decisions come to you and they're already made. I'll be driving through the night."

"I can't go to Huntsville," I said. "I don't even know what state that's in."

On this we agreed: I'd gone far enough, and now I should turn back. His path would be improvised, and following it would only lead me further from home. "There's a gas station up the road where you'll catch a bus. I asked around, it's the best option," he said. "Huntsville's in Alabama."

"I don't know where that is either." I hugged my arms inside my sweatshirt. "Okay," I said, nodding. "Okay. Should we call my mom?"

"I'll leave that decision to you."

§

The gas station was a long, neon-lit building with an all-night diner. Rick pulled below the overhang of the diesel pumps, where mosquito hawks swarmed and an automated voice played through horn-shaped speakers.

"You understand why it has to be this way," he said, clutching the wheel.

"I do," I said. "It's fine."

"You didn't bring your drawing things, did you?"

"No."

"Sometimes I wonder about if everything was different," he said. "But some things we can't change and shouldn't try." The CB radio groaned with static. He handed me a roll of cash—sixty dollars in ones and fives, wrapped up in a rubber band. "It's just you now. You'll make your own way."

"I know." By then I'd climbed down from the cab. "Go on. You don't have to wait for me. Thank you," I added.

§

Then I shut the passenger door, and Rick drove off alone. He'd kept what he wanted, which was independence, and he'd thrust it upon me as well. I wasn't angry or disappointed, because for him I was something to be tended to, and I didn't want that either. So that's where we parted, at a standard-ass truck stop some hundred miles from the town where we'd both been raised.

He and I have seen each other since then, yet to say we've reunited would be too kind. Rick Lohse is a traveling man, and the comfort he seeks is temporary. He needs a hot meal, a place to leave his truck, someone to admire the promise he once had. Then like a chick from an incubator, off he goes without memory of the heat that nurtured him. But as I say, he and I have seen each other since then. I've seen his hair thin and his boyish face become wrinkled and pocked. I've watched him defend his freedom only to suffer by his own stubbornness. And I've become more like him than I would wish.

That next morning I caught the bus out of Trinidad. The sun rose north of Denver, and my legs were so tight I felt I could kick through the scratched plastic window. On a whim, I got off in Cheyenne and ate two hot dogs for breakfast, then I took to the streets without an agenda, observing a world I hadn't known existed. I walked past statues and murals, city parks and country clubs, even the Governor's Mansion. Later on I stuffed my gym bag in a stack of tires and ran, and I kept running. It was what I wanted: to be untethered, to make my own way, become my own man alone in the face of uncertainty.

From there I retreated north, hopping off the bus again in Scottsbluff and Hot Springs and Oacoma—any place with a name suggesting adventure. When I arrived home, my mother greeted me as though I was only returning from the corner store. Days later she would say, "I suppose I never asked: How was your little vacation?" Her question angered me, and I knew our time of contentedness had begun its end.

But before that, in those two short days with Rick Lohse, I remember the early morning, when the sun was only a suggestion and the road was entirely ours. We wound south into the Black Hills, beside Mount Rushmore and the half-finished Crazy Horse Monument, on which men have labored to this day. Soon the road leveled out, the trees became sparse. "We're on the long haul now," Rick said, drinking coffee from a silver thermos. The red pin of the speed gauge tilted ever forward.

In that manner we entered Buffalo Gap, a butte grassland where bison stood not fifty yards from the road. It was then he told me all his history—running cattle and working on crews, the accidents and anger, his daughter, the creek, his loss and limitations and remorse. He cried without shame or embarrassment, and I knew these stories were true, because they were unhappy.

Outside, wheatgrass shimmered over the plains like water in a pool. Hawks flew lonely through the cloudless sky, each in a path its own.

ACKNOWLEDGMENTS

Thank you to those who served as first readers for many of these stories: Jackson Alexander, Brian Maxwell, Gilad Elbom, Caleb Tankersley, Mike Goodwin, Robbie Hargett, Chanelle Benz, and Sara A. Lewis. Thanks also to Shannon Klug, Barbara Jensen, and Lee-Ann Kastman Breuch—all from the Department of Writing Studies at the University of Minnesota—for providing selfless, abundant support. Thank you to the innumerable teachers who patience and generosity shaped the work. And great thanks to Andrew Gifford and the team at Santa Fe Writers Project for their dedication to this book.

Previous versions of these stories appeared in the following journals: "Worst at Night," *Beloit Fiction Journal*; "Don't You See?," "The Anchoring Root," and "Can You Swim?" (as "Three Little Parables"), *Rock & Sling*; "Sing Along," *Chicago Quarterly Review*; "Barkley the Ice King," *North Dakota Quarterly*; "Charges," *Midwestern Gothic*; "Make It Yours," *Tahoma Literary Review* (AWP Intro Journals Award); "Sea Changes and Coelacanths," *Whiskey Island*; "Fricassee," *Best Short Stories from* The Saturday Evening Post *Great American Fiction Contest 2020*; "In My Life with Carl Lehmann," *Clackamas Literary Review*; "Road Songs" (as "My Rig is the Wild, Wild Heart"), *Foxing Quarterly*.

The title "Worst at Night" is inspired by the 2001 Lucero song "It Gets the Worst at Night." Elements of the story "Beacon Light" are inspired by the rock band Ween. The story "Sea Changes and Coelacanths" takes its title from a 2006 double album of John Fahey guitar instrumentals. "In My Life with Carl Lehmann" derives its title from "In My Life" by The Beatles. The story "Road Songs" contains lyrics, used with permission, from the 1985 folk song "Wild, Wild Heart" by Bill Staines.

ABOUT THE AUTHOR

Joseph Holt's writing has appeared in *The Sun, Prairie Schooner, J Journal: New Writing on Justice*, and elsewhere. He graduated from the Center for Writers at the University of Southern Mississippi, where he also received an AWP Intro Journals Award in fiction. Originally from South Dakota, Holt has taught at *Catapult*, the Loft Literary Center, the American College of Norway, and the University of Minnesota. He now serves on the MFA faculty at the University of Alaska Fairbanks. Holt is an active marathoner and host of *North Star Nugs*, a radio show featuring jam band music. His website is holt.ink.

Also from Santa Fe Writers Project

Muscle Cars *by Stephen G. Eoannou*

The stories in *Muscle Cars* explore the unique and sometimes flawed relationships between men, their families, and their friends.

"Part Richard Russo, part Bruce Springsteen, part OTB parlors and Cutlass Supremes, Eoannou's debut collection is all heart."

— Brett Lott, author of Jewel, an Oprah Book Club Selection

What If We Were Somewhere Else
by Wendy J. Fox

What If We Were Somewhere Else asks its own questions about what it means to work, love, and age against the uncertain backdrop of modern America.

"Fox's distinctive characters and their tumultuous journeys will stay with you long after you finish the book."

—R.L. Maizes, author of Other People's Pets *and* the story collection We Love Anderson Cooper

Wars of Heaven *by Richard Currey*

The lives of the working class in West Virginia—a train engineer, an epileptic, coal miners and outlaws, the fragile and dispossessed—are explored in this powerful collection.

"Here are six stories with grit, guts and that old-time sense of word-sparing, stark, locomotive-driven prose-poetry that will set to thumping the heart of any lover of the English language."

— Winston Groom, author of Forrest Gump

About Santa Fe Writers Project

SFWP is an independent press founded in 1998 that embraces a mission of artistic preservation, recognizing exciting new authors, and bringing out of print work back to the shelves.

  @santafewritersproject | @SFWP | www.sfwp.com